BY RODNEY HALL

Kisses of the Enemy

Captivity Captive

Just Relations

The Second Bridegroom

Rodney Hall

THE SECOND BRIDEGROOM

Farrar Straus Giroux

New York

Printed in the United States of America
*Published simultaneously in Canada by HarperCollins*CanadaLtd
Designed by Cynthia Krupat
First printing, 1991

Library of Congress Cataloging-in-Publication Data
Hall, Rodney
The second bridgeroom / Rodney Hall.
I. Title.
PR9619.3.H285S4 1991 823—dc20 91-18507 CIP

Grateful acknowledgment is made to my family for bearing with me, also to Hall Caine and Wesley Stacey.

The Second Bridegroom

I must face the fact that you will have forgotten who I am. So if you have the patience I shall tell you. And for my part, of course, I must at last get to know you too.

I am near-sighted. My impressions of you have been those of a man who sees no details at a distance. I am given little enough to go on at the best of times. I see a blurred world of large simple shapes; as with my first view of the new land we reached at the end of our voyage south from Sydney. Looking back on it, I try to guess how this wilderness might have appeared to you.

Let me call the scene to mind. Sunshine blazes across a sea so amazing calm we hold our breath. We are in an untouched place. Stunned by sheer light—by the glare of bleached sand and the brilliant sea breaking as a white crust—I peer into the water but I don't like to mention what I think I see down there. Surely those with long sight could not fail to notice? The water is clear as air. We all look. No one speaks. Yet I would swear I can make out a sunken ship, a brig like our own or a barque. Squinting to get it more definite, I see masts and spars. Also a hull wedged among undersea rocks. Who has been here before us? What hopes are already drowned? Wind ruffles the light and the wreck is gone. Still no one speaks. They look. And I look. I glimpse a mast again and a crow's-nest. Yet they are the ones who can see—and I only think I can see. But how vivid this ocean is, with a lick of satin parallel to the coast a quarter of a mile out, like a wake and yet too broad to be left by any vessel: it is as if our whole future had already come, swept past, and gone before we even arrived. Meanwhile the past has been scuttled. A slight swell lifts that sleek ribbon and passes beneath without breaking it, like a muscle under skin. A minute later, when the swell reaches us, riding here at anchor, we rise to its gentle authority. We also subside.

This movement is not sudden enough to rock the body still fettered to my own.

The bosun had him dragged up from the squalor belowdecks and me with him, as if there was no difference between us. I am a disgusting object from living in filth and cramming my head with torments. As for him, he is not at all disgusting though he lies lifeless. Waxy white, you would think him more handsome than ever.

Can you put yourself in my place? The carcase was unstrung, a boneless weight flopping on the other end of my manacle. Such was the climax of our time spent locked together. Even after deckhands had dragged him out into the open and let him drop, he tugged me violently.

"Fraternity" rose to the slight swell with the grace of flight, her masts rocked, her idle rigging slattered. The dazzle of that peace kept us all in check. The livestock in the hold fell silent as well—listening, I suppose, to make what sense they could of the journey's end. I fancied I could hear their committee breathing. Now and again, to keep their balance, hoofs clomped down there, unseen.

As for the place itself, a rocky headland tilted and righted. The utter wild and untouched look of our new home sent a thrill through me so I felt outrage that I would soon be dead.

Two ospreys (I knew this by the way they flew) floated above and scattered reckless cackles on the air. We were close enough to shore to hear the anxious prattle of small birds among the bushes as alarm spread beneath those great shadows sweeping from one hooked arm of the cove to the other.

But the shadow fallen on me was the Master's shadow. I did not look up. I only looked at that dead fellow whose head lolled so near mine I could see it shocking clear: we were still linked by a chafed wrist and awkward arm, his being out of joint dragged at mine. But as for the fellow's breeches and naked feet, these were far enough away to belong to a man still full of life.

I confess to you that I did not care to look too long at that head.

Here in a beautiful haven, I thought, my living body is soon to be thrown overboard with his dead one. He will weight me down and drown me. Or if he don't the Master is sure to put a bullet through my skull. That is how it goes with the law. What is the difference between a corpse with a bullet hole and a corpse without? The law is for one part of mankind to explain how its oppression of the other is for the good of all. Law is a kind of algebra, in which unknown quantities are given names as simple as X and Y.

You must be aware that being near-sighted often goes along with being bookish, in my case an actual apprenticeship to a printer. Enough to say, for the moment, that I was familiar with Mr Hogarth's simple tale of rewards for diligence and that I might have hoped to end up wearing a Lord Mayor's chain of office in my old age. I was clever and quick. But such comfortable daydreams pass away, as this present dream will pass. My purpose is not to complain against fate. You will be surprised, but my purpose is to be frank. Put simply, I cannot afford to live in my past so I beg to inhabit your present.

I admitted killing Gabriel.

So now, the Master said, you owe me fifteen shillings for this man. And he let this fact settle before turning aside. Why should I waste another fourpence on powder and shot to be rid of you? he added.

I stared out at the shimmering sea, that vague dazzle, also at the empty sky. I knew then that I had not been shot.

The quartermaster came to unlock the manacle. When it would not open they fetched a carpenter. He brought his axe and at one blow buried it deep in the deck. Gabriel's hand flew off and slithered jumpy under the rail to flap into the scuppers. His body convulsed. I dare say there is little point in describing what a severed wrist looks like, budding undriven blood as dark as resin.

He shall have a Christian burial on land, the Master ordered, that way at least he'll be good for manure. They threw a length of sailcloth over Gabriel Dean's face and left him with me.

Does it surprise you to be told that the life of a felon has much in common with the life of a soldier, being spent largely in the boredom of waiting? There we were. We had reached paradise. The silver glitter of water buoyed us up—a company of twenty, as I now saw, ten assigned convicts, a master, a mistress of course, a quartermaster, boat crew and paid labour—all but one of those on deck gazing this way at the new land, or that way out to the horizon's perfect straightedge, where dark sea met a milky sky. We waited. What we were waiting for no one told us. Direct overhead the blue deepened, perfect and empty. The headland cupped us in lush vegetation.

Forest trees stepped right to the dunes at the back of a sandy beach. We waited. The sun swung vertical above. A white ruff along the sand marked the end of our voyage. Half a dozen large birds flapped away from a lagoon. They were in no hurry. They had considered the threat for some hours. As they swept overhead I recognized them: pelicans. We waited. The sun sloped in from the west, netted by treetops calling with owlish cries, lingering on the drowsy air.

Our memories have plenty in common with short-sight, don't you think?

The point was that there we floated, raiders, with no idea we were being watched.

I lived instant by instant, expecting to be punished. Beyond question this punishment would have fallen to my lot had my crime come to light at any other time. We all knew we had arrived at a new beginning. We shared a sense of destiny. With everyone afraid that the future might be founded on false hope I warranted only such attention as could be spared a minor irritation.

Still the sunken ship wavered under the water. Still nobody said a word about it. The day drew on and itself began to sink away.

I never fathomed the Master's reason for keeping us aboard until the last light. Only then, at the time when we felt most like the marauders we were and most at risk, did he order us ashore. The men looked terrified. They knew that no sooner were we marooned on this shadowy land than the sun would set and leave us helpless. We would be wholly without light unless we chose to offer ourselves as targets by lighting lamps and building a fire. So when the pinnace's keel ran against the sand not one among my brothers in servitude cared to be first into the warm sea.

What did I have to lose? I slipped over the gunwale.

I looked back. The ship could be seen but nothing of what was happening aboard until, by a small moving blob of amber, I knew the Mistress had left her sickbed to negotiate the rope ladder. She hung there against the dark hull. The current, turning "Fraternity" and the boat with it, showed me the Master's black shape reaching up to steady his wife. Did she need rescuing? He must have his arms full. Were they swaying together, staggering as the smooth swell lifted their boat; were they preoccupied with keeping their balance even on that silky sinking sea? One cow began to moo from inside the hold, sounding like a muffled herald's horn. So my moment was offered me. A gift. In the still evening anything seemed possible. Dusky golden light stood in the air. Even the little waves slapped the beach softly. I waded ahead alone, stepping up the sandy slope, aware that others would soon follow but alert to the fact that I heard no sound of them churning the shallows. Was it worth the risk of a spear in the chest or a shot in the back to keep on going, to make a run for it? Most likely I would be hunted down and dragged back by the hair, flogged and starved.

To tell you the truth, these horrors touched me only as a cold spot settling in the small of my back. My chance would last no more than a few seconds. I was out of the water and still walking. I clutched the dangling manacle in my hand and ran. I ran until a dapple of shadows confused my vision. I plunged among tall smooth tree trunks and undergrowth.

While still able to see, I must run and run and keep running.

But this proved impossible. Between death and death the best I could do was stumble and lurch. I had to clamber over logs and force my way through thickets. I plunged into a freshwater lagoon as brown as tea. Driven by knowledge of what I had done back there, letting out my fear in grunts and sobs, I was also driven to escape the revulsion I felt at the creature I had become. This was a sickness of the conscience. Reason could not help. So the choice was made for me, I accepted the chaos offered. No wonder those others did not follow: they saw the same thing. Yes, they shouted of course. But not until nightfall did I hear these shouts and by then they were mere memories, ghost shouts heard as much in the blood as in the ear.

Graft had been paid for me. Such was the knowledge I carried in among the networks of insect wings and scuttering claws. I did not know what death meant; but I did know what it meant to have been paid for, to have a grubby finger forced in my mouth feeling round my teeth, to have my feet and hands valued and my trade cited like a dog's dam. Add to this that back there in Sydney I knew one thing my new master could not have known—so craven was I, so schooled as a brute, that I wanted him to buy me. I primped to appear a desirable object.

Reason brought me to this.

Then came the chance to be free of reason itself. In the beauty of evening, ospreys gliding above, the massed confusion of the unknown taking the form of a forest offered me, on arrival here, a death cleansed of humiliation. The chaos rushed to meet me and dodge me.

Big animals fled crashing ahead through the bush as I went, leaping away, fanning out, uttering no cries but thumping the earth at every bound of terror. Parrots, catching the fear, wheeled as a screaming skein of crimson and royal blue. I escaped west towards the fading light, a confusion of fear widening in circles around me, news of my stumblings already known miles inland. While panic triggered panic those shapes remaining quite still escaped my notice. Some I might have even brushed against without recognizing them as human. Slender and dark like young tree trunks, daubed with mud and leaves, as I was later to see, they had painted each other with living earth and the fugitive design of shadows in this place. Just as the fleeing animals fled in silence, the still were still in silence.

I lay on the earth and heard the silence thunder in my blood. I dug at the soil to bury my misery but found it hard under a mulch of rotting twigs and strips of bark. I could still just see but could not go on. This was where my pride had delivered me. I looked up at the first stars beyond the crown of trees until I felt the starlight crawl on my skin.

Ants seethed all over me. Tearing my clothes, I thrashed around to be rid of them, using my last moments to blunder a few yards further into oblivion.

The last light, having ebbed away, brought me to a halt. Each minute the cloisterish dark damped and suffocated me more, till nothing but that dark was left, the infinite dark of our turning planet. I should confess, although I believe in the Bible, I accept no church. So I suppose you could never call me a religious man—and this might have had some bearing on my troubles from the start. Yet that instant of recognizing darkness for space filled me with terrified joy.

Even if the Master caught me in the morning I had won at least this for myself.

And I was the man who had brought darkness to Gabriel Dean on the previous night. Remote as that crime already seemed, this is how near it was still. I had planned the murder. It was no accident. Once he was asleep I set about my task with the only weapon to hand, because he was strong and I was weak. Could it also have been because he was beautiful and I was ugly? Certainly his arrogance showed up my humility. Beware the humble.

So darkness was in me as well as around me.

The climate in these parts being mild, I found the night crisp but not too cold for sleeping rough. I scooped all the dead leaves in reach for coverings. I planned to head inland, away from the rising sun, to put as much distance as possible between me and the coast, making the least possible noise while I was about it. This much was commonsense, meanwhile I must sleep.

In fact hunger kept me awake, the knot in my bowels, the brief dribble of burning urine. My brain, taking charge of the spirit's fascination, began to tackle the task of carving the chaos into bite sized meanings.

Even I had learned certain things about New South Wales from accounts written by various hands and from the talk among my fellow convicts. So my brain set to work on the noises presented me: the chirrups and scratchings being animal; rustles and whispers vegetable; the rising sea's rhythmical thud mineral. Further, my education helped me frame a more exact catalogue: the scratching might be small quadrupeds, possibly of a kind with rats or squirrels; chirrups, being by far the most general and continuous of the animal sounds, signified insects mating; similarly I heard large leaves being moved by the breeze, tree trunks leaning against one another to utter occasional lovers' moans, grasses whispering. Meanwhile, overriding everything, was the treetops' remote agitation. This was what kept me awake when I desperately needed rest.

At the time I did not recognize the symptoms as symptoms. Let me not appear to claim any awareness whatsoever. I had no idea I was being laid hold of by the rational world of my upbringing to battle against the allure of a thing without form. I thought I was doing well. I took pride in being self-taught. I was an idiot.

Once, from the direction of the sea, I heard men cry out in the distance. Animal, I said, and trembled.

Growing cold I diverted myself with a brief sermon on cultivating feathers for warmth and passed from the example of God's common chicken in winter to His albatross skimming above freezing wastes of an Antarctic ocean, thence to the proof of a down quilt. Again a man's cry. Had this one sounded closer, or had the breeze slackened? It made me shiver.

Speaking of ghosts: lying there on my mat of brittle sticks, I did not feel Gabriel's body twist and shudder again as it had when I was in the act of murdering him, though this was a nightmare I made ready to endure. My fear was not fear of his survival or the violence of his revenge but fear of flinching, lest I dislodge the mound of dead leaves I had heaped on me to keep my misery warm.

Rumour had it that the Master's name was Mr Atholl. I saw several fellows put themselves forward when he was picking his men, from which I deduced that he had a reputation. But there was little chance for me to form an opinion. What shall I say? He looked like any other man of substance. He spoke clear in an educated accent. He had definitely never been a ticket-of-leaver, his smell was all wrong. He appeared strong in body and a browbeater. Chained together between-decks, we agreed that the ship must be his own. And this was spoken of as the most exceptional thing about him. Beyond doubt he had a grant of land to go to. One of the sailors told us the crew were to stay and become the Master's shepherds when we reached land; there was a butcher, he told us, and the carpenter who would build the house was also an axeman. Plain that Mr Atholl intended to set himself up and stay. Plain that he intended us to stay too.

Everybody had opinions about the wife—most things I could not repeat. The fact was, we agreed, that the Master was right to be firm and not waste too much time listening to a woman's grievances. What would be our long term fate if he petted her overmuch or indulged her? That's what we asked in the knowing way of gossips who know nothing. We agreed she would only come into her own when her husband was installed on his acres and she, like the cattle, might be big with young.

I do remember something Mr Atholl told us while we

lined up at the barracks back there in Sydney—he promised we would help establish a new kind of settlement, and that we would bless the day. We saw he had bought the latest line in farm machinery when we lugged his plough and reaper aboard, stowed his chests of tools and seed, before we were manacled in pairs.

You can chain him and me, Gabriel Dean offered holding his wrist ready, I'll keep the runt in order.

That was me. And that was the beginning.

Three days may not seem long to a person in a cabin with a bunk, blankets, water to drink and water to wash in, but we spent it shut away from the light, shitting where we sat (I am outspoken because I believe you have the same scorn for the feeble niceties of language), brawling over the food they threw at us, guzzling from a drink can, scrambling for rank against rivals. Some men knew others from being in prison together. A few had even arrived on the same transport and could be picked because they dared say so little, knowing too much. Some, like me, had been in the colony less than a week and knew nobody.

The common wisdom was that transportation might be stopped at any time, that when a new Governor was appointed he would bring the system to an end, and that ours had been the last shipment. I do not know what truth there was in the story but it branded us: as if we stole some right from older hands, as if we made special claims on the future by worming our way into history.

So from the first we were treated with particular cruelty.

My dreams of the past—and we all dreamed of our losses—had skies of torn paper and little boxes filled with hopelessness. The present was something haphazard. We lived for the future. Any piracy, any theft, any evil would be made all right by the future: isn't this the truth of our colonial philosophy? I am sure you have thought about it yourself. From the Governor down to his scullery maid we became Australians, a race with one foot in the air, caught stepping forward.

The bigger this great island is supposed to be, the more it appeals to our gambling vice.

Since we were infants at our parents' knee hadn't we heard tales of fabulous lands being discovered and explored? Did we not follow the adventures of Sinbad as if we ourselves were the ones to be caught and carried by the giant roc to its nest? Tales, all tales. And tales tell a hidden truth as well as the things they seem to say.

Here in New South Wales one thing we do know is that this will be the last foreign shore, the last unknown land, the only adventure to yield none of our desires: no gold, no cities. Even the trees are strange to us and the animals are those useless freaks the whole world hears of, egg-laying flying reptiles, fantasies of Nature. Instead of taking us forward, what we see takes us back to the beginnings of time. The real and the fabulous have not yet gone their separate ways. There is nothing to prevent our fables taking root here. And we have brought plenty of them with us. One of these fables, as you shall see, had a part to play in my downfall.

I want to confess to you and to share my thoughts.

No wonder book knowledge is a good deal feared. We who have it are cursed for tying others to the past. They look down on us too, as knowing only what is already known. But is our future so different from what our past has been? And does lack of knowledge make a person bold? Here, a man like Mr Atholl may set out in his 90-ton ship, go where he pleases, stop in paradise and say: As I read the map, this bay is mine. And take it just as it is, without tales, whole in its beauty, never tainted by our sort of knowing.

You may wonder why I say such things. Let me add that in my own way I am a word man also. Many felons are handy at crafts; though who besides a printer enters into a trade with words? So I am set apart, halfway like the Master. But I do not keep my knowledge to myself. This may be why the others hate me. I am hated the moment I open my mouth and the words escape me. My workman's lilt is little help; if anything it brands me as a traitor to the comfortable sort of ignorance. The Master set the seal on their resentment when he said: I shall one day be glad of a printer and there might not be another happen my way.

So Gabriel Dean came to promise he would keep the runt in order.

There is a quality of cruelty that goes with beauty; and

not by chance. The beautiful are well aware they can do as they please. Even their victims will forgive them because they answer our deepest need. In them we recognize an ideal. Have you thought about this? They flatter us with their friendship. A man's wife may be excited by him if she sees he has the loyalty of a beautiful friend, his own meagre portion glowing in the radiance of the other. And isn't this a fact anyway? Surely it is true that, without making any effort to be like them, some glimmer of the style they have from Nature rubs off on us?

Just as I was the last to be chosen for Mr Atholl's household, Dean was the first. The Master remarked: He'll sire a pretty race built like Vikings. How much more strength the Master showed later when he turned his back on my crime, as if speaking about any lag, with the words: So now you owe me fifteen shillings for this man.

I have come to believe that Mr Atholl knew he and I were shackled to the same bond of words, words to be broken out of before the new kingdom could find its airy regions among the clutter of old misfitting uses. That's the best way I can put it. I hope I make sense. And although he had more use for Gabriel Dean than he would ever have for me, we shared another bond, as you shall learn, in our fatal ambition to be loved by one woman. Yet we were always opposites. He was a horse man and I have never even learned to ride.

So, the Master put up a fence because he feared his herds might cheat him of power by running away. Just as his little herd of human beasts, with their starved souls, might be more ready filled than himself by such gifts as the land offers.

When you put all this together you will see that maybe I did not bolt out of fear that he would punish me for Gabriel Dean's death but for fear the Master wanted to possess my soul.

That first night of my escape, as I lay shivering in a sweat of terror, the ocean booming like a cannon, I thought of the "Fraternity" and how she must be tossing at anchor. I could picture the panic on board while they made ready to take her out to sea, beating against the wind, to ride at a safe distance from the rocks. This put me in mind of the crew and cargo. Who was still aboard? Could any of the livestock have been ferried to land yet? And what if the weather obliged the ship to stand offshore for another week? Wouldn't this be the saving of me? As for "Fraternity's" human livestock, the one thing I wondered was whether they had yet buried the corpse of the only beautiful man among them. And with what words. The words interested me as always. Ah, there it was again: I will take heed to my ways that I offend not in my tongue—I will keep my mouth as it were with a bridle—how does it go?—something about the ungodly—in my sight I held my tongue and spake nothing—I kept silence, yea, even from good words—yes, that's right—but it is pain and grief to me—my heart was hot within me—and while I was thus musing the fire kindled and at last I spake with my tongue—Lord, let me know mine end and the number of my days, that I may be certified how long I have to live.

Do you know the Psalms? If so, you will see that I had this part of the service by heart ever since I set the type myself for our congregation's prayer sheet. My job was to check the spelling and correct the proof as well, and take it round to the vicar.

Of course I remembered the Master's promise that Gabriel Dean would be buried on land. But would it be the Christian service as usual (The snares of death compassed me round about, and the pains of Hell got hold upon me) or was he bold enough to let the ocean to do the talking and simply shovel in some soil while listening to the solemn drum of a swell against the cliffs?

I shivered, and thought these things to stop myself shivering.

What sort of burial would he offer me when his men came upon my body torn by snags and dead of hunger? Such were the questions I put as I lay among queer plants, my teeth chattering, hearing around me the movement of animals which ought not to be tied to the name animal. There were no answers.

When I could, I made a beginning: I promised not to try reading the messages I heard and smelled and touched, tasted and saw. I would respect them as having no use. None of them would be the same tomorrow. Nor were they the same yesterday. Each moment is the present: it sounds and smells and tastes only of itself.

I was in a fever and brainsick. Often at the source of courage lies something pitiful. Perhaps I had the fever from Gabriel. He fell ill on the day we set sail, the day he fixed me with a glittering stare and held his wrist against mine, inviting the trooper to chain us together. Was it that I dared not move, or was I indifferent? A curious flutter in the blood as I relive the moment (let me, above all, be truthful with you) suggests that I had been less passive than I thought. Might it not be that I so mistook his motive as to be proud he chose me?

Once we were fastened together by the manacle the character of this device became clear. The clasps fixed around my wrist and his were joined by a short iron bar with only three chain links at either end. When he raised his arm I must perforce raise mine at least some of the way. When I wished to raise my arm he had the opportunity of forcing his down to prevent me. By a mercy the clasp was somewhat loose on my wrist, though cutting tight into his, otherwise I think he would sure have broke my arm, so violent did he twist it to keep me, as he said, up to the mark. Even before we left the quay at Sydney he pressed against me so I could feel the strength coursing through him. And when I tried watching the swooping seagulls he fixed me with a scowl until I met his eyes. He smiled then, and I knew what to expect.

No sooner had we stumbled into the steerage of "Fraternity," hearing cattle protest under the floor, than he used the iron bar of the manacle and felled me with a terrible blow. Then I was hoisted to my feet and cursed for a clumsy fool.

So began the tortures. Had his energies not been sapped by illness I doubt I would have lived. With each assault he delivered a homily against idle ways. The preacher's tone of these good offices afforded the company such amusement that a deckhand was sent to ask were we Frenchies and begging for a taste of the cat?

Do you begin to see what kind of life I faced? The blood dried on my cheek and my hand was caked with blood. Gabriel Dean invited me to throw my whole weight against his arm. Yet I could not shift it. For a moment I comforted myself that this victory should appease him.

What is the point? he snarled.

Why were we not Frenchies? one asks, looking back. Why were we in this miserable hole instead of out on the streets and burning our Bastille? By what right of Nature was it not myself but Mr Atholl who seized a thousand acres of virgin land with the assurance of doing the crown a service?

The manacle had FJ stamped on it. The blacksmith who forged it wished to be known by his workmanship. I had to carry it with me when I escaped, of course, clutching the bar in the hand fettered to it or else have it bang painfully against my leg as I ran.

I clutched it long after I had fallen among the tangled bushes and burrowed into my bed of dead leaves.

You must imagine me, on that day, once I felt safely clear, lying low, seeing nothing, alert to the sound and smell of the wild. I confess that I prayed: Only let me come upon water in the morning, Lord, and I shall not complain. This was the last time I prayed to the God of our childhood, the stone dragon at Kirk Braddon, and the first prayer of mine He ever answered.

Just as I will end my life here in the newest British colony, I was born in the oldest, the Isle of Man. Not until my father's time were we out from under the heel of the Earl of Derby, styled King of Man.

Think of it. Jesus Christ himself might not have scorned such a title.

Mere words, you may say. Did the dragon need a title to strike fear in the hearts of our folk? Well, as to the matter of words, I am the one who knows. The law—I mentioned this in my previous letter—is for one part of mankind to explain how its oppression of the other is for the good of all. England and Scotland wrangled over the Isle of Man. Scotland and Ireland wrangled. And then Denmark and England. Finally, between England and Ireland, it came down to science: was the island (being midway between them) hung off the English coast or the Irish coast? Lawyers got busy and came up with a proof as good as any. They brought serpents and toads from

Cumberland and set them free. When these creatures flourished and began infesting the island the law accepted this as proof of British sovereignty . . . the fact being well-known that neither kind of vermin can survive on Irish soil.

It all comes down to soil in the end. And we know our own, which will someday be ours entire.

What was it that I heard as I lay on the ground under my heap of shifting leaves? Tiny things. I believe it to be true that those of us with imperfect eyes have keen ears and keen noses. I heard crawlings and slitherings among the roots. Sounds you might have missed. I was still sobbing and gone in the knees while the jungle crowded over me. The muddle of terror, without let or way, was as bewildering as that world of leaves. Yet listening to the tiny sounds, I found my panic began to give place to calm. I could neither see anything nor do anything. I must accept what the world sent me. Serene now, I reviewed such facts as I knew: that the denizens of the Antipodes were flying squirrels, hopping fawns, insect sticks with the wingspan of a hawk, scorpions able to stand upon two legs and bite their victims as well as sting them to death, owls with horns, and water badgers half-bird half-animal. The lags on our transport talked about huge herons without wings which could kill a man with a blow of the leg, snakes spitting poison darts, giant ants and man-eating spiders. I thought of our Manx dragon at home, our four-horned rams and tailless cats.

So what would an Englishman choose to fear if that were the coast he had just landed on for the first time? These were the fears of foreigners. No doubt our folk were monsters too, of a sort, with a language which we kept to ourselves and no other nation could make head nor tail of. My father never spoke a word of English, not even to curse the Earls of Derby.

So I lay and shivered. Wind rushed sudden among unseen trees to sound like gusts of approaching rain.

I will never be found, I thought, I am in the most secret place on earth. Perhaps no human foot has ever trodden here. Perhaps no poet has attempted to tell of its real monsters. Yet the night noises, apart from that rising wind, were tender. Cheepings came to me from every direction so that I thought of them as a web of fairy bells. I listened, as enchanted as a child.

I heard a man.

So this was the true monster. My heart had no doubt of the matter. He trod cautious. Twigs cracked under his feet like they had under mine. But he had control and stepped with care. There was no terror in him as he came. Only in me. His long pauses were proof that he was listening. He listened as hard as I did. But perhaps he had good sight and this would count against him: his ears less sharp than mine. I could not hear him breathing, only his feet nearby. Nor did he curse under his breath the way I had while I ran in panic to escape the Master's hirelings. He stopped. He came on again. Yet I was right:

I could never be found. Might he trip over me? No—a chance like that would offend against Nature and the natural disorder. I had control of myself. Then I heard him away to my left. And again farther off. What if it was some other large beast of prey? Some meat eater pausing not to listen but to scent the air? This I had not thought of while I lay so calm of a sudden. The joke is that, once he was gone, he took with him my feeling of being safe.

Did I sleep? I do not know.

Towards the middle of the night an unearthly light crept into the bush. Lying there gazing at the treetops I was astonished to find that what I had taken for a dense umbrella of leaves showed itself as frail lace. Close by my face, where I could focus, starlike growths sprouted around me, and glowing fungus. Even the plenteous dead leaves matted on the forest floor each had its own shape when brought up close, its honed edge, pointed and curved. They were like lily leaves afloat on the dark planet. A spider hung silvered in her web. And a radiant veil of harmless insects flew past stretching and retracting.

I tried to recapture my fear in the name of commonsense. I, who at the best of times could see nothing sharp beyond reach of my hand with its dangling manacle, peered into the night for signs of movement among the trees. I was expecting a threat which moved. It never crossed my mind that there might be danger in what stood still. You could scarce blame me; don't we all picture the hunter running or stalking or pouncing? Hunters who stood fixed, doing nothing, were no possible threat because they had not yet been imagined. So, although I suffered a feeling of being watched, I remained too ignorant to care. And this saved my life.

Before dawn I dropped off several times. Better than the previous night aboard ship when I had no sleep whatsoever. So I woke refreshed, the sun about to rise behind me. If the lacy moonlight had given me back a lovely world, those few moments before I staggered to my feet and shook enough terror back into my head to drive me on showed me a glimpse of heaven.

Some few birds had already woken. They talked more than sang. Their messages were disagreeable, the most persistent being bantam-squawks. A mouse, I could plainly see its furry shape, scuttered among leaves still warm with my warmth. The surrounding scene resembled a tangle of grey wool, perhaps a witless weaving. Mocking me from right above my head came a terrifying cackle. I leapt to my feet, drenched with fear. I stared up, able to make out nothing other than branches and foliage spread against a sky pale as whey. The sound did not come a second time.

The truth was that since there was enough light for me to see by, there was also enough for the Master who hunted me. I listened. Other bird cries happened like stones knocking together, accidental. The light strengthened. Then the first songbird, high above, opened his throat and gave out penetrating notes strange as the man I once heard sing alto in the "Messiah."

Do I surprise you? I want to surprise you.

At this signal a great tree branched into fire! The forked trunk, still solid with night, tapered up as bough-shaped tongues of flame. The breath of happiness caressed me, smelling of the sea. Parrots swooped among glowing sprigs.

The day was already my enemy. I knew I ought to escape yet I could not deny myself the simple marvel of this burst of rosy light as it steadied and strengthened to brilliant gold and the whole top of the tree shone like a hood of jewels. Hints of blue swept through the air above. Even at risk of being noticed I watched until the marvel faded. A firming wind set the forest in motion. I was caught in a mesh of sound, netted by slishings and patterings.

I looked around. Morning had come. It might be my last morning and I knew this. One could see quite well. The dense tangle of dead and living plants wove a single messy tapestry which hung right before my nose. There seemed no foreground or perspective, just a simple up and down without any way through.

Away behind me a cow lowed mournful notes of warning. There could never be an instant's doubt as to my direction. Not only must I keep the risen sun behind me but I must escape the constant ocean's muffled bass drum.

When fear took hold it was more desperate than ever.

I ran, stumbling, up to my ankles and sometimes up to my knees in the mat of fallen branches, peering at vague threats, betrayed by the great hubbub I made as I went. But how else could I go? This was a country where stealth was an art that must be learned. Hopeless to bother with it now. So whatever blundering speed I could manage must give me a better chance than ginger care. You know how it is in a forest: as you run, the nearby trees sweep past you, a bow wave arcing around on either side, while beyond them an outer band of trees moves your way (as the moon also goes with you)—so the quick trunks flee behind while the contrary trunks beyond keep pace to trap you at a standstill. However desperate you attempt to escape, all you can ever do is speed up this confusion and drive the counter-circling mazes faster.

I flagged. I gulped and gasped ratchets of breath painful as punches to the chest.

Both the near band of wheeling forest and the outer band counter-wheeling slowed down. When I stopped they stopped. I was a beaten man. They were trees in a land never used. Some memory of clocks ticked loud in my brain, I swung round—expecting to surprise my enemies as they closed in on me: the Master with his whip, felons slavering at the bloodhunt with murder on their tongues. Nothing. I saw nobody. Only the standing-still blackness of tree trunks and the pale grey and fragile pewter green of that sky-to-earth tapestry.

How difficult it all is to describe.

The frightful cackling laughter started again, after a gargle at the beginning. This time two voices laughed as rivals, their mimic mirth struck through me so that I felt cold, helpless to escape, helpless to decide which way to go or how to hide. I saw a pair of plump brown kingfishers glide down from a branch above me. They swooped toward a glint of metal on the ground ahead, dipping through matted growths. Vines with blunt hooks at their joints ripped my rags to remnants.

This glint was not metal. Let me say that I now believe metal is as alien to this land as beasts with hoofs. The glimmer came from a strip of still water. Perhaps the smell of this water was what the cow went on about back there at the dunes. I thanked heaven. A few minutes spent drinking here might save hours later. Thrusting my mouth in I sucked a bellyful. The taste, brackish and slimy, was delicious. I raised my wet face and the breeze blew cold all over my skin. Had this drink been fatal—the delay a minute of flight I could never have back? Fear got at me again. I was sweating and my knees trembled. I struggled up. I had to make good. I began to believe that, against all odds, escape was possible.

The black tree stumps ahead of me were not trees at all. Dumb with terror I swung round to bolt the other way. The black tree stumps behind me were not trees either, though they stood still as rooted things and old beyond the span of human generations. I had been trapped by weirds of a kind no book of travels ever described.

Neither Sinbad nor Prester John came across such a breed as this. They had eyes and the eyes watched me from under shadowy brows, but they did not have proper faces or torsos; theirs were face-shaped clumps of feathers, and torsos of leaves. Nor were their arms ordinary arms, because the white bone appeared to grow outside the flesh. Where a man would have cock and balls some grew a thing like a melon. Where a man stands on legs they stood on a single prop. But though their heads kept as still as their sprouting bodies, the bird-eyes fixed on me moved when I moved, stopped when I stopped.

We were relics of ancient life suspended in the amber morning, for I include myself.

I heard cattle mooing, then a distant shout. And so, by the enquiring tension they centred on me, did they. One of them unfolded a second leg from the single stalk he stood on: he levelled a weapon at my belly, a blade made of bone by the look of it. He stepped toward me.

The menace of magic made the menace of British law and its bullies look bland by comparison. On my legs, arms and scalp the hair stood stiff in shock, I can tell you. My skin cringed. The creature holding his sharp bone stepped through the tapestry, treading where there was no floor, out of the vagueness, gliding into focus and showing himself for what he was. He had black skin, shiny on the shoulder but folded lateral across the chest as if tucked and sewn there. By the wrinkled belly I judged him quite old. Stringy arms were knotted up with veins.

Between the toes of one foot he dragged a spear along the ground. With no warning, he stuck the blade in among his head feathers. Straight after that he flipped the spear up into his hand. He balanced it, a simple sharpened pole with no metal head, the tip steady, inches from my throat. In the other hand he held a flat wooden paddle with patterns cut into it. There was menace in this also. On the paddle lay divers items: a smooth white caterpillar appearing powdered with ashes, a tiny yellow plum, a leaf with three points, a pink mushroom and a root like a misshaped parsnip. I looked upon these articles, upon the paddle, the hand holding it out to me, and the wrist growing clumps of foliage.

I could see now that his entire body sprouted coverings, mostly clusters of feathers in a narrow continuous line beginning at the neck, branching in two to fringe both collarbones, looping down on either side to the elbow, back up to the armpit, looping again down to the knee and back up . . . until at the belly button the line around the left side met that from around the right. So these tufted feather lines drew the silhouette of a dwarf on the body of a man. You will forgive me mentioning his gender, I hope. I wish to speak as frank as possible at all times. His cock and balls hung unadorned amid dark hair. On this fellow's face and head were such masses of plumage that all I could distinguish of normal humankind were moustaches above a wide mouth and two piercing eyes fringed with fluttering pink down.

In the eyes, which I expected to express raw evil, I saw the most unlikely thing, a flicker of terror. Yes, and I could explain it: my blood-guilt must in some way be apparent. These were creatures sensitive enough to death to smell it on me already and to know me for a murderer.

Water dripped from my mouth. The manacle dangled against my leg, reaching the ankle. My freedom had lasted less than twelve hours.

Despite my father being determined that I would not be hag-ridden by superstition in the form of God or omens, I believed in one fixed rule: that action of any kind will be punished. I had escaped execution, so now it seemed I must die by poison. Let it be. Amen. Without hesitation I reached out and took the fruit. Bitterness dried my tongue. Pips stuck to the roof of my mouth. The creature made no sign of approval. I took the leaf and chewed that also, tough and stringy though it was. Numbness dulled all sensation around my teeth, which were never good. Still he held out that decorated paddle. Next I accepted the mushroom, which was now clearly a toadstool with gills the colour of cream, expecting this to be the quickest acting poison but surprised by the delicate smell it had to it and the lingering taste of pepper. The caterpillar I could not stomach. I told him I was refusing by shunning it with my hand . . . and then offered it to him, because the truth came in a flash that death by a spear through the neck must be more merciful than death by corruption of the vitals.

From all round the circle low cries were uttered, sounding like amazement.

The next of these strange beings to unfold a second leg also stepped forward, feathers and leaves set trembling, and took the caterpillar between finger and thumb with elegance enough for Lady Mary Montagu. He put it in his mouth and chewed. Odd, I noticed that the hairs on his legs and arms were bristling like mine and that every bare patch of skin was tight in gooseflesh.

From down at the beach came the whinny of a frightened horse, reaching us like a call to the heart, confirming what I was. One day and a night after I had committed murder, my conscience at last took control of my fear. The law was now justified in treating me as a convict. I could never again be innocent in my own eyes. My sufferings to that time had in all probability scarce begun. If you look at the idea of Hell, the truth of it is that no suffering can be enough once guilt is admitted. The guilty are hardened. Only the innocent feel true anguish. My murder made good the judgement passed upon me a year before.

Perplexed at what could be done, I did not move. No more did those feathered beings. My death would be too simple a way out for both of us. My death as a murderer did not balance Gabriel Dean's death as a bully. This was the ceremony of it.

They knew everything.

Wind rushed among trees, bending massive branches,

tossing a sea of leaves and causing a scurry among our feet. I had reached the hub of chaos.

The great sound made of a million tiny sounds was ruptured by words: Get at him! Do you see where the bastard went? By Jesus!

Sticks snapped, menacing snorts could be heard to the south of us, boots tramped not far off. The circle of feathered creatures remained still as God on their single props. So did I at the centre. I knew then that I was invisible. We listened while the chase approached in a rush and then passed away through dense scrub, returned, turned, split into a shout from in front and two shouts from behind. We heard the snorts again and shuddering breaths. So it was a horse that had got loose, after all! Something truly valuable. The whole while, the air ringing with interruptions, the remote ocean thudded. How familiar it sounded in a lost land—that unhurried heart of the world—the exact same sound as I remember from childhood.

Only when the marauders could be heard no more did we begin to move. I can not say whether the circle of figures around me took the first step or I myself. Whichever, we were soon stepping light. I have already described how the forest baffled me when I tried to run, a band of trees to either side moving back the opposite way and the far trees moving with me; just so, these weirds moved when I moved. After the first shock, I gave way to my fear. What use to pretend being brave? I made an offering of all pretence. I began to suspect that the fierce cold laughter high among the trees had in fact come from within, perhaps from the region of my navel. Also that the twin voices mocking me might be a single voice going one way while its echo travelled back the other, as the voice of a dragon is said to be two, both in the one throat.

Twigs crackled under my feet but not under theirs. Only the whip of a sapling bent aside now and again and springing upright marked the air with their passage. They stepped with bird feet, dipping their toes among hazards they were used to, dancing ahead on sprung thighs. Always they kept the circle complete and I began to find the going easier. Inside my head rang those alien words of English: Get at him bastard by Jesus.

I realized that what I had taken for murmurous foliage was the speech of these creatures. Talk flew among them, alighting on one and a moment later on another, till it took up a rhythm. The pulse of the sea drifted into their mouths and out again as chanting. We reached a ridge and began loping across more open ground through waist-high grass from which tiny birds dashed in a mad scatter of alarm.

I had arrived at a place where all my knowledge was useless. The joy, as I found myself filled with it, could not be described, the pepper taste still alive on my tongue.

*Season upon season of smoke fol*lowed. Billows rose from that cup of land around the bay and drifted inland, carrying like incense. We wandered, seeing the smoke from afar as a mushroom on the horizon; or from the edge of the scarp smelling it mingled with seasalt on the wind; or as we returned stepping through patches of it caught among vines and star-flower bushes.

I had now lived with my spirit beings for long enough to be convinced they were men. From time to time they cleaned the feathers off their skin and shook out their long hair. Admitted, whenever they approached me they did so with ceremony, but as soon as they felt at a respectful distance they fell to chattering and bursts of laughter. Loneliness tortured me. I could not learn one single item of their language because they seldom said anything direct to me. I was beyond words.

Only on rare days did I see them dress so elaborate as they had at that first meeting, patterns of mud tufted with leaves and fluff disguising their real shape, though there was one time when they pranced around me on a grass slope, each man with a cross strapped to his back and held firm by a belt made of hair. The crosses were very tall things, spindly and wavering, and two or three times as tall as a man. Where could they have seen the crucifix? How did they know? Yet there they were, nodding crosses, painted with bands of colour and having bunches of leaves like a dead hand dangling from each arm and a third stuck up for a bush of hair at the top. These weird crosses swayed around me: something between a pilgrims' parade and the type of gangling sinister figure we used to see at Douglas fair when acrobats on stilts stalked in among the crowd. They kept it going until night seeped up out of the earth and swallowed the men entire while leaving their crosses to move this way and that, outlined against the sky. The moon did not come up at all that night. I expected the cold blade at any moment, I can tell you, a bone knife between my ribs.

At an early stage of our travels they took a dip in a pond and stood up all streaming. Their shoulders were glass and their wide wet smiles full of simple pleasure. Frogs croaked from the margin where I stood. But a terrible fuss broke out when I made moves to join them. Some shrieked, some covered their eyes, others messed up the water as they came churning out to cut me off. Little did they know how amiable I was. Not for the world would I trespass beyond the limits they set me. To my surprise, I realize now that I showed their taboos more respect than the taboos of my own folk. Such curious creatures we are, to be so fascinated by discovery, to have such a passion for things we can collect as items of strange behaviour. My protector—this is how I think of the guardian who first offered me poison—brought a wooden dish of the water for me to drink. A scarlet dragonfly darted in and hovered over its glinting rocking surface. For a moment I held back my thirst, waiting for the insect to dart away before I set my lips to the rim. By then a tremendous silence had fallen. The frogs themselves were struck dumb. The pool listened.

Even during that precious moment, which might be fatal for all I knew, I was aware of smelling smoke from distant fires like an omen. As well, I had to fight off memories of home and winter by the open hearth.

The light in here is very poor. I trust my writing is clear. I was always praised for my hand. I have to keep rubbing my fingers, so I shall wait until the morning grows warmer and the sun is really up. Then I shall write some more.

Now: let me explain about the journey I began to take. These Indians—and how queer the word sits with them—were on a quest, determined to keep moving but at the same time calm and refusing to hurry. The men and the women kept separate in two parties. I could hear this distinct, the low voices and the high, though I did not catch sight of either. In all my time among them only once did I see a woman—but more about that later. Most nights their songs and laughter reached out to me, punishing me further with desolation. Sometimes one or other would let out horrid screams, and each morning early they could be heard moaning in a choir with a sound like soft bagpipes. Often, in my circle, I came upon a mess of footprints pointing in all directions, also the remnants of two separate feasts. Each time overwhelmed by sorrow, the air around that place seeming more buoyant and touching me light as breath.

No matter how far we walked during those first months we could look back and see smoke clotting above the trees or smudged out along the far away sea.

So my spirit beings were human. That is the point. And while I decided not to intrude on their perfect chaos, routines already began to eat away at the grandeur of it. I even caught myself giving them a general name: Men. Well, the excuse was to hand, this was cleaner than clumsy dodges with roundabout words, which would lead to an even greater plague of English spreading in a world which English has no right to. Do you see what I mean? I hope I do not offend you with these ideas.

I began to see what order is. Order is a way of trapping

anything wild, tricking us into the game of thinking we understand. When you come down to it, the need for order is the mark of a coward.

So each of my saviours was a man—and I prayed I would not be forcing them into a frame too rigid if I thought of them in secret as Men. It was Men who brought me food, food I ate with a will. Lengths of snake, roots and stalks, berries, bleeding hanks of meat in a crust of burnt fur. But not those pale fat naked caterpillars. They ate the caterpillars with gusto but never again offered me one. I came to the point of believing I might rather fancy trying the taste but I did not ask. First because I was too timid, then because I was afraid to risk the calm of my boredom. You see how quick our fears can be dulled?

The boredom loomed so great—and so much like a thing—I had to give it a name also. I called the boredom Hope. I had two words, then, and between them the span of daily life: Men and Hope.

Yet at first the days were never the same. We walked unknown ways, the water had a different taste each time we drank, we fed on such food as could be found, we slept amid undreamed dreams. The one thing that did not change was that if I made an independent move, even for a piss, the Men rose up around me in that silent circle to watch what I was doing. Each night we slept in a different spot except for the time when it rained eleven days and I was allotted a cave overlooking a river which flowed through a plain where herds of kangaroos flew toward the hills as the shadow of a swift dark single cloud.

This went on for weeks and months, through seasons of cold and seasons of heat.

Then one evening we heard a familiar rhythm, every eight steps we took: "Boom." Another eight steps through undergrowth: "Boom." The scent of the wide sea pricked my nostrils. As for the smoke, well perhaps a year had passed, so it was little more than a stale ghost of what it had been. Ah, with what longing and surprise I found myself back where I began. To be near the sea! The sea runs in my veins, of course. I feel as sad near the unseen sea as I feel near an unseen woman.

We came to the ridge and climbed it on the western slope. You must imagine that, without knowing, I had become a forest creature, faulty sight no longer a hindrance, having learned to feel the ground with my feet. I saw with forest eyes used to the gentle forest light. Indeed, I wondered whether my eyes might not have strengthened. Well, from the crest of the ridge the sight was blinding and so strange I could make no sense of it. Dazzled by all that brightness, I found myself looking down at an assault on the earth itself beyond anything I might have been ready for. The natural aspect of the place was wiped out. The soil gaped with lacerations. Alien to itself, the land lay wounded. From just below our vantage point a road, cutting between the dunes and the ramparts of forest, curved north as a giant scar. Dumps of stony rubble were heaped here and there to either side. Above the road stood tree stumps sawn short and charred, and whole ghost trees. Lopped branches and shattered logs sprawled at odd angles. Away to our left a few horses, penned by rough yards, browsed in the warmth, standing in various fixed attitudes, ignoring the two fellows in hats (this much I could make out) who plodded along the road. Down to the right and closer at hand some roofed dwellings were set square to the road, the grey sheets of roofing being bark or thin-cut shingles. They were lashed down with beams and rope. You may judge how this astonished me. The walls were slabs and in all probability thick enough to last out the century. Other roofs were visible through a patch of bush. From one of these a puff of smoke stood up. Breathing air fresh from the sea, I could not believe so much had changed in so little time. When last I set eyes on this place I was running through it, tripping and crawling, cursed by my own fear, expecting any minute to be caught again and dragged back to be chained to another murderous bully for the term of my sentence. Since then, that dense mat of undergrowth and close-set trees had gone. Wiped out. Raw earth lay open to the weather.

Please do not imagine I have forgotten what civilization is. I saw the road clearly as a road. The buildings as buildings. But I also saw, with the sight of Men, the horror of it, the plunder, the final emptiness. My protector looked around, long and searching, then turned to the others. But they could no more explain what they saw than he. I felt the puzzle as they did and even some of their fury as my own.

What is this for? My lips formed the question from the shock I saw in their eyes. Only later did I wonder at not feeling any longing whatever to go down and be part of the honest work of sawing timber, ploughing and sowing the fields.

Instead, the sheer scale of violence made the sight hard to grasp, so out in the open it was, and so ruthless. A glare of sunshine beat on the whole houses and the broken soil, exactly as rain must have slapped down on them a few weeks before. It looked to me as if certain patches of the road might still be cut with troughs of mud.

So what was this for?

I answered myself as I might answer a child: to produce food. Although I had little doubt that the Master's sheep and cattle were somewhere nearby, it suddenly made no sense. As I saw it, he had taken a place, complete in itself, full of the food I had been living on, smashed it to fragments, then slaved at the work of carving out something in its stead, something different. But—how can I put it?—something no longer complete. His enterprise struck me as cross-grained if not downright contrary. Do you see what I mean? Does it puzzle you too?

As we stood looking, the sound of an axe came from nearby. Soon two axes were working. A ringing "thwok" "pok" told how big the tree was, just as the rhythm gave away that they were working at a single tree and not two.

The Men turned together to look to the south-east, agog at what confronted them down that way also. A spidery trestle stood out from the cliff—a landing-stage with a boat moored at the end, doubtless the pinnace because it had masts. Tucked inshore of the pier a kind of loose raft jostled slow and heavy in the shallows. This I recognized too. It was a jam of floating logs. Here the road ended.

I want you to come upon it all as we did.

"Fraternity" was nowhere to be seen. I thought of the deep water in the channel out there and the rigged ship I believed I saw underwater, standing intact with masts and spars, and I thought about us and what queer folk we are to be murdering and drowning for the sake of a quest after some paradise that can never be. A terrific conflict raged in my heart. I knew the risk, supposing somebody saw me there, but I was drawn to it. One day there would be a new town here.

Put it this way: I was living a life in which I did nothing for myself, indeed I was not allowed to do anything. If I had I would have offended them and their hospitality. Suppose I reached out to pick one of the berries you could eat: my guardians would call warnings, block my way, break it off for me, place it on the ground and smile when I took and ate. Though I longed to wash and to swim when we came to streams, they cried out in shock at the least hint that I might try. If we had to cross to the other side they made me lie on long poles, covered my face with a mask of reeds matted with mud, and carried me on their shoulders.

Of course I objected, but what good did it do me?

I contrived to parley by simple signals. We knew this between us. My right hand I used for subtle messages such as coaxing, a request for eatables, to signal pain or doubt. My left, with the manacle still hanging from the wrist, I kept for warding them off or for messages of power. In an emergency or when I felt helpless rage I got hold of the iron bar itself and shook it, the chain and empty ring clattering about on the end, and brandished it above my head. They also took my meaning when I turned a shoulder on them. Such were the rituals, and I only ever addressed my protector or, when he was absent, his deputy. In any case no one else in the circle had looked directly at me since I turned down the caterpillar and passed whatever test they had put me to. They kept their eyes cast and I obliged by gazing a bit to one side. Like being a king, such manners held my interest for months. I was engrossed in myself and my state. Let me say I had no interest in keeping count of how long elapsed since I escaped the Master because I never wished to leave the Men or go back to slavery. This way I soothed my guilt on account of Gabriel Dean, clear that I would never need to face a court of law.

And yet you may be sure the guilt gnawed at me. The torment of it, constant and dainty, did much to fill my life in the dumb solitude I was condemned to.

During our journey they pointed to every feature of the landscape as if I might recognize it. They behaved like family welcoming a cousin who has been many years away from home, reminding him of childhood games, making a tour of certain caves and standing rocks. They took me to admire particular trees with nothing remarkable about them, gnarled growths and even strange shadows on the soil. As I soon realized, they were never pleased when I showed the least surprise or wonderment. I was only able to gratify them by gazing long at what they showed me and seeming to recall it. How did I do this? Well, one gesture was to place my power hand across my mouth, the manacle banging against my chest. Then their occasional talk would quicken to a chant. I knew the exact game, I became an actor, I played the part of showing gratitude for treasures I had never thought to see again. Having lost so much during my life I could feign this easy enough.

You must forget that I was ever a plain felon assigned to a settler who might be called Atholl. I was the centre of the wandering circle. I was the one who had to be protected from being seen by women. You must imagine this: me as the shell of a dumb brute standing under the last of the uncut trees, agape at that loggers' road connecting jetty and farm.

The fellows in hats unhitched a couple of horses and swung up into the saddle. They came riding along the road.

At this, the Men exchanged wild looks. Leaves bunched on their wrists trembled.

What shall I say about the sound of horse hoofs coming near? They took me straight back to Kirk Braddon and the Douglas road, to my dear father and brother fastening capes around their shoulders, rustling through the kitchen and hurrying out into the night to meet the horsemen—whoever they were—then setting off on foot to a secret conference with others of their trade. Each time they met the horsemen they risked being caught. At very least they were likely to be away for a week, during which my mother would fret, strong though she was, and hide her tears. Horse hoofs on a soft road will always take me to the heart of my grief. Also to our morning vigil at the stone with the dragon carved into it. My mother had me believe the dragon would return in glory when the Sassenachs were driven from our sacred shores and their brand of Christianity with them. She held my father to blame because he took Hall with him at these dangerous times and because he was what she called a backslider in the faith, not giving himself to politics and rebellion, but only to adventures which she scorned for being mere scratches on the skin, as she put it. And there was some suggestion in her tone, when she read me Bible stories, of a commander teaching his scouts the enemy's language.

Close though the riders came I could not see either one clear enough to know him. They passed beneath us. Peculiar temptation: to shout Help! Or what if I dislodged a humble stone with my toe? Fear and longing raged through me. The ocean pounded in my breast, in my head, in my throat. This was exactly as I had felt when I slipped over the gunwale and knew my chance would not come again, that I must cut and run up the beach or be a slave for the term of my sentence. I was two persons, both cursed.

In my terror of being caught again I wondered if the Men might be planning to hand me over. If so, I could not raise a finger to defend myself because I was feebled by an unbearable ache to reclaim my right to belong in the hateful familiarity of meanings. No need to feign this.

Yet I was tugged in the other direction by pride in my new grandness. I, once terrified of being hurt by the manacle I wore, now struck terror into others by simply shaking it above my head. Was I to give this up for the sake of sentiment? The point is that neither the terrified person nor the grand person seemed to be me. I could no more accept myself as a convict than as a chief among Indians. Even the real murder seemed too tricky to grasp. I still found difficulty in believing that I had done this, that I had fully intended doing it, and that when successful I had felt proud and jubilant. Likewise, deep inside, I could not believe in the fetish thing I had become—despite the fact that I was quick to understand how to behave towards the Indians and despite the fact that day by day what took hold of me was a hallucination that this was indeed my natural birthright and that I really might be recollecting what was already fixed in my nature.

A separate matter was the fear of further punishment. I had been called a coward and I dare say there was some truth in it. Standing silent at the centre of the circle of invisible Men, I belonged among them. I repudiated those colonial fellows (what a great Biblical word "repudiated" is). To cry help or dislodge a stone and attract attention could only bring the wrath of both parties upon me. If I did not die immediately by the spear I could look forward to being hung by the neck from the mast of the pinnace.

There is a flock of birds outside the wall. They are setting up such a hubbub they must see something I can not see. It is a grisly reminder . . . being shut away again. How do I help myself crying out and asking why you leave me locked in here? Well, I suppose you are giving me time to show you the whole truth.

That day the shifty sea trembled right out to a fixed horizon where the hot milky sky rested heavy on it. Two osprey shadows flickered across furrows and upturned tree roots. Nagged by anxiety, I worried about what would happen if the Men recognized where I had come from, with whom I really belonged. They might see in me the exact same thing I saw in those fellows on horseback down there!

When at last the truth hit me, it hit with full force: the Men had gone. Alone, I stood marooned between two lives.

I looked down along the new cut road at those approaching figures. I watched until they passed below me. Horses' rumps glossy and tails swishing in a remembered way, they rounded a bend among the treetops at my feet. Out of view, the beasts could be heard plodding on in the dust. They stopped. Why had they been reined in? I listened. Why? That moment the strangest sounds began: a wooden crate from another world being dragged across a warehouse floor, some huge disaster shrieking, the splintering crackle of glassy air splitting from sky to earth. A frantic wind puffed round me while the crown of leaves behind which I hid rushed away, breaking a passage as it went, followed by a colossal thud. Birds scattered from the felled tree, birds like those whose feathers I was given to stick in my hair, tiny blue fly-catching birds, pink-crested birds, even a hawk. The air was still full of the rhythm of the axes which had already stopped. Away from the shock a kangaroo fled, crashing past without a glance at me.

A curious pressure around my leg called to mind subtle memories. You must imagine it rising to my knee. And me, discovered there, understanding everything too late. I remembered: this was the clasp of a snake! Who had I become now? Never was escape more urgent.

What was that, then? demanded a voice below, while the kangaroo could be heard still breaking its way to safety.

I am expecting the savages, said the Master, we are

ready. If that's you up there you can come for a dose of medicine, you heathens!

I heard hoofs among the stones and the two of them walked their mounts back till clear in sight and not more than a dozen yards from where I stood. The escaping beast still bounded away into the distance, heading up the slope as I had escaped an age ago—splintering thickets. The snake reached my thigh. There it hesitated. I saw the head waver as it investigated my manacled hand. I dared not look again. I dared not move. But I had glimpsed a twist of rose-red underbelly, glitters of sunlight on lustrous black scales, and pinpoint black eyes. A tongue flickered against my skin. I felt the snake's coils glide higher to use my power arm as a route for reaching my shoulder. The Master and his servant stared right at me. The snake's head examined my head. A comical thing came to mind, that snakes are famous as being nearsighted.

A shot, fired like a single clap, sounded ridiculous. There was no harm in such a puny thing. I stared at the Master and his levelled weapon, then at his companion. They stared straight back up at me. They were so close I could almost have spat at them and expected to find my mark.

Heathens! the Master sneered. And his trunk sat so firm he seemed part of the horse.

The other's hat nodded.

Only then did I realize an amazing fact. They were

looking right at me but I was invisible to them. My snake rippled up over one ear. The rasping scales gave me the shivers. Into my hair the thing went tunnelling. The tail still reached down to my feet. A slender creature this was, filling me with nausea and pride.

If I am King of Men, I told my coward fears, then this soil is my soil. Toads and serpents belong here.

From down in the direction of the felled tree the long stroke of a saw began, rasp, pause, rasp. One of the horses stamped. Time enough elapsed for a war to be fought.

Or was I mistaken? Could the Master see me? Did he ignore me as not worth his anger? Did he think I was a decoy, to be left alone until I lured his true enemies within range of a bullet? Grief dug deep into my vitals. The pain grew unbearable. To be despised by him—an individual I thought less worthy than myself. I had to challenge him. Yes, this pride had hidden in my heart ready to betray me at the moment of my second escape. Was it possible to resist? Nature don't answer to reason. I was in the grip of forces beyond a person's control. Fate favoured me in my turn. My mouth opened and I shouted.

No shout came; only a gasp of something stale.

I swallowed to get my voice back, the voice which I had scarce used in all this time of being King. Why had I not at least sung songs to keep the faculty? Disuse robbed me of power. I tried again, but the snake came coiling round my brow.

I don't suppose we hit the swine, the Master grumbled.

The eggshell head (can you imagine the frail skull of a snake, so like a bird's skull?) swayed while checking my open mouth which, very slow, I began to shut.

Didn't catch any screams, did you? the Master laughed short and slapped his heels hard against the horse's flanks, moving off at a trot. A few extra words reached me garbled by the wind. The long saw continued rasping to an even stroke. A minute later the riders emerged again on the track above the floating logs. I could not tell which way they were now looking but they soon passed beyond the jetty and out of sight.

I was full of becoming invisible.

Rigid as a stick for fear of my dangerous snake, I made to turn gradual, seeking help. You may imagine how slow I turned and how hope leaped up in me when I found the circle there again, each man perched on one leg and the leaves tied at his wrists gently rustling. Their eyes would not meet mine. I came to the point. I could understand that I may as well give up hope of ever being helped. I was marooned in grandeur or in shame (it scarce mattered which), made untouchable by my struggle against fate.

Once you live by the rule of order you put yourself at risk if you are green. You can not win. The court proved this to me: I was transported for forgery to confirm the matter. My father denied there was any such thing as law or any such thing as smuggling. He treated his courtroom like a Punch and Judy show. My mother told me he scoffed at the judge and farted when the jury brought in their verdict. But I only remember the wooden way he stood up there to hear his sentence of death . . . plus the curse he put on them.

In my case the courtroom was to be just as strange to me but, without the good humour my father's courage allowed him, I wallowed around, adrift on a nightmare. Expelled in the dock, I had to face an old schemer dressed in silk and animal hair who never let me speak when I needed to. He kept cutting me off for breaking rules I did not understand. He had a mace carried around and set up in front of him and he talked in code. I had to crawl to him by calling him My Lord. As for the constables, the Oxford beadle and the clerks, they formed a ring around me. I was trapped. And I trapped myself because I did show them respect, my stammering a tonic to them. No doubt they enjoyed seeing me pale and scared. How easy it is to admit the truth to you! But at the time I had no idea a trial has its roots dug far down into the murk of our savage past. This time my mother could not be there. She knew nothing of what had happened to me. None of my kin were there, nobody from Kirk Braddon or even from Douglas, to watch the end of my bright hopes. I was just a cheeky boy, I suppose, jeered by the public with their Oxfordshire hee-haw.

So you are a skilled tradesman we hear? That is how the judge put the question. His voice went like honey.

We do not question the quality of the work you were trying to sell! You assure us that this is a forgery and your own forgery. We shall not attempt any comment upon the art of printing in case we show our ignorance! His wit was greeted with general merriment. However, we are puzzled, he went on, as to why you have called nobody to give witness to your mastery of the craft or your good character, not even your father. We should hesitate to call you a bastard, he said. There was lots more laughter. Oh no? You don't say so? How very misfortunate—was it for smuggling we hanged him?

The country itself was hostile.

All my life on our little island I smelt heather without knowing it. The cry of seagulls and the sea's distant beat were in my blood, but how was I to know this until I no longer heard them? When at last the time came for me to tell such things the courtroom fell silent, even the scratching pens stopped while the clerks listened. I got going all right, so much so that I warmed up to the crimes of the Earl of Derby's family and the Scots before that, of Irish kings and the Danes in their longboats. I did tell them about the heather and lost cries on the wind too, but not about the dragon cut in stone. The name of the dragon was on my tongue but I held back. Nor did I say I had a brother named Hall, because if he was alive he would certain to be hiding still.

We shall not deny you the music of seagulls, never let it be said, Judge Mitchell assured me from under his wig of a sheep, you shall feel most perfect at home in respect of gulls and squalor. I am sure His Grace, the Earl of Derby, will approve. You shall be held at Wapping until the first available hangman can carry out His Majesty's pleasure. Accept my regrets that I do not know of any heather at Wapping!

Where a grown man would have reacted with rage, I was still so much a boy that I just felt indignant instead. This was the first sentencing, before I appealed and they commuted it to transportation once they admitted my crime was only forgery and nothing worse.

You see how I wish you to know all there is to be known. My shame is the very last thing I ought to keep from you. I shall come to the tale of my appeal in good time, but let me confess here that even when they clamped me in irons aboard a transport bound for New South Wales I kept myself lofty. So pure and bold I felt.

As to the matter of the forgery, there was no dispute. I had planned it, set the text on the press, gauged the lead to a niceness, and paid due respect to the great man whose sign I copied—simpleton that I was and eager not to fall below his standard. I locked the type into the forme, ligatures snug and firm, painstaking in the matter of ink, worried lest it might not be as black and even as the real article. I started the coffin gliding to and fro. When there were enough copies to choose a clean sample of each sheet the practice runs were burnt. My crime called for skill—and love of English. You may guess that I felt confused on this score. Loyal as I was to my father.

My father spoke no word of English in my hearing ever. Manx was his language and he stood by his own folk. He was neither for the Goidelic people nor the Brythonic people: the fact that Irishmen and Scotsmen could make little sense of our tongue being proof enough. As for the English, how should poor father even know the law when he had no word of their rules in his head?

My mother it was who first taught us, Hall and me. She was quite another case, being fixed that an education meant the skill to make headway in life.

I should not want the lad's wife one day to accuse me of condemning her to the poverty I've had myself, she once said, so if he turns out to follow his father it will be because he chooses to and not from ignorance of any option.

As a girl she had been known to the Bishop of Sodor.

Your father may say as often as he likes, she told me, that we should call him the Bishop of Sudr-eyyars, but in my view that would be contrary. Sudr-eyyars is a name more proper to the dragon than either the Church in London or the Church in Dublin.

Being green (again) aboard ship brought more trouble. I had not imagined there would be allotments of power even among the condemned, privilege and rank. I was to learn that the rigid order of society is mirrored even more rigid in prison. The constable had his fellow bullies among the felons, like the judge had his fellow sneerer. Just as a nightwatchman ought to be cautious in case he offends against a bailiff's territory, so you can trace a ladder from such as myself on the lowest rung up to a murderer with the dignity of an Earl of Derby . . . only that the Earl has more anguish and more spilt blood to answer for than any petty copycat of the bottom deck.

I was green even on the quay at Sydney town in the bright drizzle of a new place, a stranger to the ropes. Again it was my downfall. When the gentlemen arrived to look us over (does this call to your mind a particular scene?) I myself was insolent enough to look over the fellows I was mustered with. One commanding figure, a man moderate tall, of solid build but lean, still bore about his stance the independence the others had lost or had had whipped out of them. Simply to see him look the gentry over, quite the way they looked at us, gave me heart. So very green I was, I jostled among the ranks to a place at his side. Putting myself as low as possible on the ladder, do you see?

I would pay the price.

My sight again played me false. Once beside Gabriel Dean, having elbowed my way among lags showing no interest in the draft, this ideal rebel revealed his nature in disagreeable details: hard mouth, cruel eyes and a manner of flaunted coarseness.

Did he need some creature to cringe and adore him?

Well, I was this creature. When those who were chosen to board the "Fraternity" were chained in pairs he offered his wrist alongside mine. We were joined together.

I'll keep the runt in order, he promised.

Saying this, he was speaking sidelong to the Master, as I have come to realize, marking the difference of their worlds by claiming a likeness between them. From that moment the Master would see how the matter stood among his felons: whom he must reckon with, and how vigorous a chief convict might act to force others of the serving order to obey.

I was nothing to Gabriel Dean. He didn't even need to look at me to tell why I was there. But once we were chained together his coolness showed as hate. I had served his purpose and he bristled at being yoked to me for three days. No sooner were we aboard "Fraternity" than he knocked me to the floor and, with one arm, hoisted me to my feet again. This was not for my benefit, I was nothing already, but for the others'—to show that there would be a vacant place beside him for the right candidate, for a lieutenant. Like his counterparts in society he had the vanity of cleanness and kept as free from filth as conditions allowed. But contagion is a thing unto itself and mysterious. No matter how the strong man twists or turns to avoid it, if it is in the air he breathes or in the water he drinks he is even more prone to contract an illness than a weak person—such is the divine law which levels everything—because he consumes more air, more water, more energy. Such contagion was already at work in Gabriel Dean. To tell the truth, he might have known this. He might have staked his claim when he did to get in first while still able to impress the rest of us, aware that he would recover quicker for not having to waste his strength coping with rivals.

At most an hour after we weighed anchor, the ship creaking into a steady swell, his bare arm against mine felt sticky with sweat. Having no time to lose, he smashed his chain in my face. He set me humiliating contests against him to prove that the effort of my whole body was not enough to match the arm I was locked to. He forced me to foolish gestures when he raised his hand and mine had to follow it. He refused me the simplest comfort of resting at ease by jerking so violent as to wrench my shoulder out of joint, not to mention more disgusting offences against my pride. This is enough.

By the second day, when the fever struck him severe, he was already warranted as our leader. I had served my turn. And yet there was a smallness in him so that he could not let up. I suppose he feared the fact that I knew for certain what state he was in, whereas the rest might only guess because being so few—just ten of us in steerage—we had room to spread out. This, added to the lack of any window, gave him the cover of poor light. He kept up minor torments, seeming satisfied as long as he made me gasp with pain. I dare say the thud of his blows impressed the others and confirmed the glimpse they had of my bleeding mouth when that hatch cover had been slid open for a voice to roar: Are you Frenchies or something, begging for a taste of the cat?

The third day he lay there, for the most part, inward with his illness, so absorbed by fever he took no interest in anything else, not in food, not even in tormenting me. A curious awe fell on the company. We began to hear the noises around us, not just the timbers under strain from the sea, but anxious animals in the hold bellowing and barking. The passing voice of a seaman, brisk about obeying orders, bare feet running across the deck above. Once a woman sang out, but we could suppose little from her tone except that she was displeased, though we held our breath to hear. Her accent declared her to be of the Master's company.

I thought about her. I tried to put a name to her but I could think of nothing new enough.

During this break I had leisure to take stock of what lay before me. Mischance had already marked me out for the butt of malice. Once free of our shackles, it would be anyone's guess how many lesser bullies might jostle me as an easy and proven victim. Some I could fight, but most were like to find me as weak a prey as they wished. To think of it robbed me of manhood. I had a loser's heart. I slumped there. Meantime Gabriel, that fastidious ruffian, grew inward and slack. He snored while still awake.

An idea came to me.

Once the idea had come, many hours passed before I could take it in and hold it up to the light of reason. I felt knotted by doubts at what it would mean. You will laugh, but I even took into account that, as a man wronged, I had my pride and that acting on this idea would damage my good name. I have never been hasty. You may be surprised to learn this. But the habit of care had bred in me a custom of reckoning risks. In such matters I am used to being correct. With this in mind you may not now be surprised to hear that I valued my own notion of honour. My father had been a gallant man and an example. I asked: Did he die deceived in me? Were his affections so misplaced? He once said to me (though the poetry is lost in English): Being your mother's son will load you with enough to live up to for it to last a lifetime.

My mother, who made an enemy of Christianity, taught me the Psalms. We may not be church folk, as her saying went, but that need not mean we are Godless. That is how she was.

Are you ready to hear more about my crimes and not dismiss me as a rogue? What have I told you of my first offence, for which I was transported? You should not forget how hard I worked at it: I studied the document, set the type myself and checked each careful flaw to get it right, slaved over a tiny chip cut in an upper case H, the precise irregular lines, also that I went in person to the dealer in Oxford to sell it: my "Commentary upon Twofold Victims of Fate in the Thebaid of Statius, from the Press of William Caxton, Anno 1491".

The funny thing is that I still have little idea what the Thebaid of Statius is or what it might mean. It is just a name for a book. The original, nothing to do with Caxton, had been put into Irish from the Latin. This much I know. And I can recite the opening by heart, having tinkered with it for so long to get the print right. "This tale of Thebes was written in A.D. 1487 at the House of Fineen, and in the same year died Ua Mael-Shechlain, to wit, Laighrech Ua Mael-Schechlain, son of John, son of Felim, son of Ferral Blind-eye Tiernan." I was in love with the music of that. I used to chant it to myself as I trudged home on cold damp evenings. The commentary listed four items to be dealt with: twin heroes, the divine beauty of women, the death of a dragon, and a voyage to an unknown land. Each item had earlier echoes in Celtic beliefs.

Going back to the most ancient times before history there was a Goddess who took two bridegrooms each year—have you heard of her?—one for the winter and one for the summer. Each had the task of killing the husband who had lain with her for the six months before him. This idea could still be found, so the commentary said, under the skin of the Thebaid of Statius, enemies in pairs and friends in pairs. A warrior having a lion's mane, with a warrior whose bushy boar bristles rise like a horror of white-shrike wings when with wild angry terror he seizes his enemy. So in our Celtic tales the Goddess chose a bridegroom with a horse's mane for summer and a bridegroom with goat thighs for winter. The summer one twanged his bow to make warlike music. The winter one hooted through the cold dark of our secret self. Just as the Thebaid of Statius has women grey-eyed and distinguished like the Goddess, so our tale has a Goddess like a woman, crimson cheeked, crimson lipped, with fine calves, slender feet and rounded heels. In both there are fiendish mad monsters loosed on the land to devastate it—I wish I could remember the whole thing to tell you it word for word—monsters part serpent, part clawed beast, and journeys to strange lands.

Anno 1491, by the bye—did you notice?—the eve of Columbus's voyage to the unknown.

The commentary explained that the Christian imagination had refined those beasts of fable to achieve the glory of unicorns and other marvels, as listed in a forged letter from the supposed Prester John, beasts not content with being beasts but mixing the virtues of many kinds. A forged lion with parrot's feathers. Forged horses blessed with horns for use in battle. A magical bird of fire called Yllerion which made a habit of plunging into the sea where mortal birds, sucked down by the high wind of the plunge, drowned while Yllerion rose again like the Goddess, flaming up through the waves to fly into heaven. A pretty story. This Yllerion could swoop boldly on an armoured knight, catch him and carry him off into the clouds, complete with his horse, and eat him there.

So we fancy what we do not know. We dress what we desire in gorgeous hopes. And our ancient stories curl round on themselves to bite their own tails.

I was a simple boy and carried away. I did not miss the fact that this Thebaid of Statius, whatever it meant, was translated first into Irish and only then into English. For every reason I was determined to do a perfect job.

Can you want further proof?

I already knew about the Goddess of Kirk Braddon taking one husband at the feast of horse mating in spring and the other in autumn at the feast of goat mating. An old lady, a friend of the family who helped with our Melliah, many a time told tales of the kind, with the Goddess gorging the lust of each new husband while she got him ready to meet the death he was chosen for. (How he must have fought against fear of his coming death—and yet, would he not in truth be excited by the ritual also?) Storytelling is a great thing where I come from.

The Goddess still lived in the Isle of Man when Vikings began their raids. Each summer the longboats swept in. We needed leaders to beat them back. The stench of burning villages rose on the wind. Common folk were in fear of their lives. The time came when a horse king, who proved himself the hero of a summer campaign, stood tradition on its head. At his execution he fought back and the new winter king, in white goat skin, lay bleeding on the soil. You may know the story. The ritual had gone wrong. Christians were among us. So we became the nation we are. The past was dead. The Goddess lost her power. The age of kings began. There will be no end to wars until a second bridegroom brings back the peace.

My mother mourned the fact with the old lady. I suppose all this lay somewhere behind my choice of what to forge in the first place. However the rest of the island may think, we of Kirk Braddon were still the winter king's folk. I myself once heard his flute in the far distance on the night of a new moon. I heard it here too. Yes, seated at my table, blind and helpless in the dark.

By the way, I have opened the biscuit barrel. I do not mean to steal but I must live. I ought to record the strange crumbling of a biscuit in the mouth. I can think of nothing like it. Already this biscuit is itself a journey back to some strange place where I have been in dreams. I find myself hungry for the sharp taste of a beetle I know and the numbing juice of a green leaf.

Did I tell you about the forest and how, while I was escaping, I lay body to body with this warm unknown land, gazing up through the treetops at a shimmer of moon lace? Of course. And how freakish birds whistled and cackled?

Each day, escorted by the circle of guardians, I moved among charmed hills as I moved among my questions. And I saw with joy how disordered they were. Food was brought me without any need to lift a finger. Drink was brought. We left the place of the little water badgers with duck bills and webbed feet to set out for the place of winged squirrels. We found giant footprints where a two-legged creature had walked and left the ripped relics of a native dog to die from lion-sized bites. A passage through the forest of shaking treetops could be watched while the creature itself escaped being seen. Down through a gully he went, violent in his haste and invisible as wind, up and over a mountain.

If my names for these marvels do not convince you, this is not to say the marvels are not there—simply that English has nothing to know them by. I do the best I can because I want you to understand that there is something to be understood out there, something free of the law, free of any comforting faith in a God whose motives may be explained through our own, something that has become the map of my heart.

At last, I have dared confess! And don't you see? If once we gave things our own names we would have to begin destroying them.

Rain rained. Hail hailed. Frost froze the ground. Trees shed long rags of bark. Creeks ran and stopped running. Flowers opened to the moon. The sun grew hot again. Short nights bristled with mosquitoes. The earth baked hard. The water they brought me tasted of death. Still we walked and we slept in the open. Sometimes we paused on a mountain where the empire of leaves beneath us was all the same strange hue, not quite a green nor a brown nor a grey, but closer to green than anything else, leaves cloaking range upon range of foothills where hot air danced like a million daytime stars. At another stage we walked out from the forest shade to a grassy plain. Clay-yellow grass, silver at the tips, up to our chests and level with the horizon where tall mud spires stood, from which the Men dug termites for my dinner. Another time we reached the ocean, ginger on the sharp rocks among salt water pools, the damp air a blessing to my tormented skin. Feasting on lobster we heard the women, gathered just around the point out of sight, splash and shriek with happiness. Nothing was more foreign than this happiness, nothing was less English.

Once, we saw a ship under full sail standing away to sea. I could not make out if she might be the "Fraternity." She headed south. My guardians watched her with dread. The great sky (and I believe you will accept that the sky here is wider and deeper than anywhere else in the world) showed us lessons in emptiness or shuddered with thunder or filled the mind with swiftly floating clouds. Skies drained white by heat. Skies glutted red with blood. Skies pink beyond the morning mists. Skies as a black field sprinkled with soft daisy stars.

A few times in our wanderings we came upon signs known to me but not to them. You may guess how threatened the Men felt when we discovered a shirt hung from a sapling. Imagine the witchcraft of a copper nail, or the imprint made by a cloven hoof! The knife we found became a sensation because I wanted it and was set on having it. I signified this by drumming my leg with the manacle to clear them from the spot and picking it up for myself. In the same way I put on the shirt to prove I could turn blue. They moved back a step. Perhaps they expected me to disappear altogether in the sky. The copper nail I lodged in my matted hair.

One more thing about coming upon that knife: the sight of it surprised me into feeling a surge of joy. Yet the important thing now was that I could not let the joy show. Joy was too human a thing. Impassive, I bent and took the knife with my power hand, then stabbed at my own leg to prove its point. They observed the trickling blood, also when it stopped and crusted over. Having nowhere else to carry the knife I jabbed it in through the fabric of my shirt and out again, hoping this crude loop would hold its weight.

The Men watched to see how I would use the knife and the nail. But I kept them to myself as too precious even for the ceremony of death when one of my guardians died. He had been stalking a kangaroo. We watched him glide in the squatting position with only the top of his head above the seed-level of the tall grass, when he vanished of a sudden. The quarry went about its quiet business. No spear whirred from the cover. No hunter went leaping to claim his kill. We found him twisted in a struggle against nothing, face etched with frightful pain, and an ant already at work on one open eye.

It fell to me to mark this serious day with my own ritual. And I did have the service by heart—or at least the right Psalms, as you have already been told. Strange that the first words of English I ever spoke in the presence of these people began with the text: I held my tongue and spake nothing; I kept silence, yes, even from good words; but it is pain and grief to me.

The sound of mumbo-jumbo, said out loud there in the wild, made me appreciate the dignity of it. Well, so much for the Order for the Burial of the Dead. I did explain that I once printed it, I hope?

After speaking, I wondered what might happen if I produced the knife and cut a lock from the corpse's beard to see what they made of that, because I still knew nothing about them really. I thought thoughts of using a stone and hammering my nail into his skull. I thought of sacrificing my blue shirt to wrap him in. I did none of these things. God's words were enough, in the event. The circle moved on. Still at the centre and still untouchable, I was taken from that place as I had been taken from so many other places. But this time, once I was out of sight, people back there began wailing a chorus of long-drawn wails. One voice sounded like the dead man's own. I paused to listen, certain I recognized him. They let me stand.

Are you curious about how readily I threw in my lot with them? But did I, I wonder? Yes, because I felt so contented among them.

For their part: who was I to them? You see, in their way of looking me over and agreeing about me, there was what I can only call deep familiarity. This was a fact as tricky as quicksilver. At all times they behaved with perfect confidence that they knew who I was. Even when we came to have some sign language between us they did not ask me to explain my coming among them. You would think they had expected me, they were so little surprised or puzzled.

Can it be that these people have refined the notion of brotherhood among all mankind until they take no thought to defend themselves, nor even to display curiosity? What is society, at bottom? Must there be fences—some people inside and others outside? The closer a family grows, does this mean that anyone who is not kin will be all the more unwelcome and kept out? If so, how far may kin be said to stretch: to second cousins, to second cousins' spouses?

This sort of conundrum teased my brain while I walked in my cocoon of silence at the centre of that charmed circle, hearing nearby laughter and snatches of forbidden companionship. For my part, so little idea did I have of them that I still can not say if they even saw one another as individuals. Most duties they did as a group.

Yet if I ever tried to solve these issues by applying the question to myself I came up against the fact that I did not know my own answers. At the centre of our family were my parents—but could two people be a centre? My father had certainly been head of his household, but how often was he there? My mother, being born with a different surname, might have thought she belonged more to her father's family than ours, yet she was the anchor, the one we depended on. Were there two intersecting circles? Only two? In my father's line all the eldest sons took the Viking name Hall: so when had that circle intersected with the Celtic circle? And how about my Uncle Fox, mother's brother, also the jolly young woman he wed—didn't this confuse another circle with the two we already had? And so forth, until I reached a halt at the boundary of the entire island, the Irish Sea. This, surely, would stand as a limit to my belonging? But many a person went over to Glasgow to try his luck, or Liverpool, or Belfast, or even to France. So wasn't the sea itself enough, then, either?

Following this line led me to some pretty claims, until I recalled the Englishman who, unwilling to believe I had the skill to deceive him with my forgery, accused me of stealing the genuine article, a national treasure . . . which straight away branded me as a foreigner. I was too young then, though it is most likely less than two years ago, to dispute with him on that score. I had to accept exile to avert the worse disaster of being hung. So much for the brotherhood of man!

Then, if we grant the view that, as humans, we all belong within the one circle, how can a person ever be in exile? Add to this the extreme strange fact that when the British cast me out to the remotest strand on earth, the natives of this place—part man, part plant, part bird—recognized me, set their lives around me, and made room for the mystery of my being there in their routine day.

How did they feel kinship with me considering my clumsy ways, though? When we travelled they moved among the tangled plants without the least inconvenience, seeming to walk straight through a confusion of boughs and vines woven together as if on purpose to resist any attempt at pulling them apart. They paused, polite enough to check on my difficulties from time to time. I scrambled after them, forearms guarding my eyes, head down like a bull, cursing and panting, breaking a passage by violence and ill-judgement.

Yet, of course, they have their own circles.

I soon learned that the men and women travel and even camp separate. I longed to see how the children were reared and whether they took all men for their fathers and all women for their mothers. Having never fathered a child and being fearful that I never might, these were the times when I felt sorriest for myself.

I was still in my own childhood. All I ever learned of the deepest bonds I learned as a boy, as one who receives and has little power to give. Then here I found I had become the giver. Granted, they supplied my food, but

I was not bound to accept it. Nor was I bound to do anything I did not choose to do, provided I remained within the circle.

There you have it. I hope you are not laughing at me. Like any other king the symbol of my absolute power was to be useless. They adored me in their way. The fact that we had no speech in common warranted my greatness, you see, and their need to serve me. If I had been able to make myself plain how could they fail to see me as a man like themselves. I was wholly alien: therefore, to the marrow, I belonged.

The Men kept me as their King.

I can not yet say how I should address you. My hand is trembling as I toy with Dear . . .

Do you remember how red my hair is? The beard I grow and my chest hairs are the same bright colour. I have heard it said that hair is dead already, a dead part of the spirit being pushed out through our skin. My hairs were all I had to lose at one time, so I collected them. You will think this strange. Perhaps I do too. But it saved my life as you will see. Each hair that came away in my fingers, complete with a tiny bud of root, I rolled together with the others, using a little mud, to make thread. There was no plan in my mind when I began this work, but as the thread thickened to cord I thought it might one day be useful. I rolled it round my power wrist and tucked it under the lip of the manacle. Besides being safe there the cord served to dull the pain which never let me go. The new comfort shocked me because it proved that I had not let my spirit be broken. So I was not even wasting the body's failures.

The murder had been an earlier proof that my spirit would not be broken. The murder had given me back my courage and turned the beatings into a victory. Yes, to look back after so long, seeing myself dragged on deck while deckhands carried the body, seeing us both thrown down before the Master and reading disgust on his face, was also to see what the behaviour of the other lags meant. I did not notice at the time. But those chained felons, who crept two by two into a brilliant morning and turned their backs on the dazzling sea, watched. What they watched they watched with respect. They saw the carpenter come and kick that splendid body to clear enough room for his skill, then cleave the wrist at a blow. Fool that I was, I missed my chance; stunned with the guilt of the thing, I failed to see what the Master meant.

You owe me fifteen shillings for this man.

If he were squeamish, Mr Atholl would scarce choose New South Wales in the first place, nor would he be in possession of a large land grant from Lieutenant-Governor Snodgrass. No. And it was not only me he spoke to about the fifteen shillings, he had meant this for everybody. At last (and too late) the meaning became clear. It was a contract, wasn't it? He was saying, All of you are here as tools to be used while I carve out greatness for myself because beyond the vision nothing matters a damn—so whatever you cost you must pay back.

My fifteen shillings debt was to raise me to the leadership Gabriel Dean claimed when we set sail. That was a good man, the Master's words meant, so this must be a better: worth fifteen shillings extra.

The truth is that I need never have run away.

One day we followed a creek for hours, clambering up from boulder to boulder and reaching a high valley where the air was dim and green as lichen. Here we came to a forest of ferns so tall we walked under them among the bristling stems. The ground was covered by rocks spongey with moss. I wanted to rest and enjoy the song of one or two melodious birds in that quiet theatre but my guardians knew that we had not yet reached the place for sitting. Further we went, among darkening leaves, till we seemed to have pushed our way up among the treetops, lost to any sense of direction. Then we broke through, clear of a sudden, right into the sky. The land opened below as a stupendous gorge. I felt my soul fly straight out of me and high above the forested hills so thick with the screech of a thousand cockatoos, launched into that valley of space.

Do you see it?

Such a place this is, with the sides of the gorge like long winding curtains of rock hung with ropes of white water here and there. The cascades seem to fall too slow and to defy nature, the far ones are heard like a long sigh in an organ pipe beyond a soft thunder of those nearby, while above everything countless leaves whisper supreme. You should bear in mind that I was living in the close and always changing places of a plant world. So now the vast and simple space with its vast and simple sky transported me into the life of pure light.

I know how an eagle feels.

My soul aloft, I could even render thanks to the dull past for growing thick upon me as feathers. I cried out. How shall I explain this for you? There is a word, but like a fool I can not be sure how to spell it! How embarrassing that my spelling should let me down when I most need to say what I mean. Exstacy (extasy?) was what lifted me up. But now I feel an idiot trying to call it to mind and set it down. What I discovered was that pain, even by itself, can be enough to carry the body in flight. Out over the killing emptiness I soared. Gliding on fear, the pure strength of invisibility holding me up. The wind my ally. Absolute confidence came to me. My guardians stood locked in their roots with the ground. I was alone. I welcomed the truth of it. Even as a child I was alone. Although Hall tried many times to break through, he could not. I suppose I hated the way he tolerated me. He was my hero all right and my friend, but he was already a man while I remained a boy. So of course he could not reach me.

Stooped over my printer's masterpiece, handling some precious vellum I had found in the stacks, inking the type for an even black and hearing the bed rumble on its sliding base, while beyond and above the workshop our town bell clanged twice across the square, cursing the lamplight I had to work by, eyes watering and wandering with strain, what else was I but alone?

What else am I, squinting as I write this, believing you are out there but not knowing?

At the gorge I could feel the actual world under my fingers and my own part in this world. I knew that a single doubt, a single lapse into worrying about some separate detail, would send me tumbling down to my death. Above, a true eagle watched as it went gliding, aloof but curious. Did I spoil his chaos? Was I a miracle in a world which could admit no miracles without losing its sense of being whole—or was I the invader who upsets an organized plan of food growth and food taking without understanding it?

The monotonous murmur of leaves and rushing water held me there.

Cliffs far down in the valley dropped into the green foam of more forest. Then I was dropping too. In an instant the world turned over. Yet I would not surrender, I would not put the name of cowardice to my cowardice.

Back among the guardians, I was leaning desperate against a bluff, fighting the vertigo which drew me to the brink. The odd thing was that even then I put it to myself that this was how I would one day come upon love.

Months later we reached the selfsame gorge from a different side and in winter. A still sea of mist lay in the vast space. Nothing moved. The slanting light of early morning showed the cliffs as a council of giants. This time I stepped to the very edge and dropped a stone, watching it hit the cliff once and bounce out into white emptiness, the tiny sound of impact as clear in the air as ringing glass. Silence rinsed my soul. Colossal breakers of mist rolled noiseless to collide with these shores.

Do you know what I promised? When I am ready, I promised, I shall step off into this and be part of the silence. I won't utter a murmur. I shall be gone.

As I write, a leaf has fallen on the page. It must have been caught in my hair. When I look close and bring it into focus, I see shape and I see colour: a curved dagger, and a riddle of green, green lying beneath a sheen of grey. If I break it open I expect I will find the blue of sky inside and the mottled brown of an eagle's feather. The scarlet stem, where it joins the leaf, branches into three—two outer edges as fine as scarlet thread, the main one a central vein. What does it feel like? Tough and velvety. What does it smell of? Ghosts. It fills me with longing. I have broken the leaf and hold it to my nose. I want to go back out there. The tang clears my head. What joy that I have found the means to sit and confess this to you.

I knew my guardians would see that I was planning one day to step off the edge. And yet I knew also that the silence included them. They watched as part of the silence. With their genius for such things they were also part of the emptiness. They could see my thoughts all right. They stood among the trees, each one carrying a bunch of leaves like this leaf, ready for the ceremony of rattling them when the need arose.

What can be said on the subject of the Master's wife? So we come to the brink indeed! Without ever seeing her eye to eye, I know what I need to know. And I knew from the day we embarked. She existed. She grew so strong that she left no room for anything else. More so when I escaped. The forest put me in mind of her. The mossy rocks. The gurgling creek. The bursting into light. The world silence. Flight. The eagle's eye. My mind was fixed on her. She haunted every moment. She had begun to be with me then, you see. Had begun to torture me. She kept off, yes, but that did not help. Her being remote was part of what made my heart leap. Wasn't I above clouds already, commander of space, able at a single shouted word to shatter that immense calm and bring the whole thing to centre upon me? So proud I was. So much a slave.

Do you agree that power, to be power, must be employed? This is why God, the image of power, ought not to be confused with Nature. God punishes and God rewards. Nature is neutral. I understand that the greater the power we have, the further removed we become from enjoying the use of it.

My guardians had power over the clan and I had power

over them. Because I was so powerful I could do nothing. The mark of my power was to not even meet the people I ruled or know how things stood with them.

Let me put it to you that any man who is a slave to love can not tell whether, to other eyes, his loved one is handsome or plain. Nor can he tell this for himself until she shows him how he is to think of her. In the meanwhile he must wait.

What else can I say? This is what all my letter writing is meant to mean.

PS. Note that my migration among Men has itself been a circle.

Not only did we come yet again to that part of the coast where I first waded ashore: during the final few days we made haste to get there. In all my time among Men they had shown few signs of haste before. I could see no reason for it now. The weather lowered and brooded but the food remained plentiful and the water good.

My mind, I suppose, was elsewhere in any case. Lately I had been puzzling over a new question: Why had my guardians never grown tired of me? Surely they will rebel soon, I thought, against being isolated by my isolation? Surely there are other things they would rather do? Surely they have had enough of this scabby foreigner and the servitude of feeding him? But if any such grumbling passed between them in secret they kept it among themselves. That got me going on the subject of good manners.

Can you see that this might be the highest human accomplishment, good manners? There is a lot to it, a lot more than sitting up straight and saying please.

Without letting any feelings show they fetched me my food, my water, watched over my nights and from time to time presented me with a black snake. The snake would be put on the ground and then they would watch with great interest to see which direction it took. They never caught the one which saved my life because none claimed me or tried using me as a tree.

A week passed after we left the grasslands before warm damp winds blew in on us as we entered the forest and fine rain fell, gusts of it being pushed in billows among the tall straight trunks and tasting of the sea.

I felt stronger than ever in my life. There was a toughness in me that I believe even Hall might envy. My skin, though a crust of sores and festering, no longer tormented me. Even my eyesight seemed a degree sharper. Maybe this was the freedom from close work; and close work had always fallen to my lot owing to my excellent vision at that range. Or maybe I simply no longer felt tense. By this stage I was without any fear of what was around me. Long since I had given up peering into the fuzzy tangle of the bush anxious because I could make out so little or be sure of distances.

I trusted the circle with my life.

We journeyed seaward, climbing small rises and strolling down long saddles. The soft weather had a promise of summer. All this took me back to a memory of the life I led long ago on the Isle of Man: I was happy.

Then we came to a fence. Imagine it. The fence baffled me as if I had never seen one before. Most likely I cried out. The Men would certainly have no name for this thing so I gave it the name I had brought with me. Fence. But what would happen now that the world of dreams—where fences belonged—began to trespass on the existing world?

My subtle hand touched the hewn rail. This was the hand, you remember, able to signal dealing and falsehood. Like a blind man's fingers checking a forgotten face my hand checked the fence. The post was a crude job, squared with an adze. So it came about that the word adze required the object adze. My fingers said yes to the adze and yes to the fence. But not me. I felt a sudden flood of anger because our way was barred. Oh, we could easy climb over or duck between the rails, but what sort of answer was that?

I thought: I have given up everything to be as I am now—helpless. So by what right does anyone come along and tell me I should look after myself again? Or, to put it the other way about: by what right does the old taint that I am worthless come to shake my new composure in being supreme?

You yourself may judge me too, for all I know, and argue that I did little for myself. But this would mistake the appearance for the substance. I had been wholly alone during this time, perhaps amounting to two years, as I say. The point of my place among the Men was that although I gave signals upon which they might sometime act there was no give-and-take between us. What I did, they observed. What they did, I observed. That is how we were. (You can see that I would need to have been a fool not to note by this time how and where their supplies of edibles were sought.)

So I stood, confronted by the old lack. The fence brought the whole horror home again. The symbol of my power was nothing but a manacle which I prevented chafing the skin by stuffing my own lost hair under it. I must have looked no less nonplussed than the Men. The fence marked a boundary across changed land. Grass inside the fence, though it might look like grass outside, was not at all the same: that grass was Property, as this was Nature. Trees had been cleared from the paddock. And the soil, yielding a lusher crop, was being fertilized by cattle. The cattle eyed us over the fence, their great heads turning to follow each move we made.

Up to that point the Men were like adults while I was like a child. Now we were all children.

There were ten or eleven heifers. Behind me my guardians waited to be shown what this anger of mine meant and how one dealt with devils. When I was little I once asked Hall what he would do if he met our Kirk Braddon dragon in the flesh. He said he would ask it to light his pipe. The monsters, stock solid on four equal legs, faced our way. Who could miss in their glassy eyes suspicions as luminous as the dusky sky? Who could fail to be alarmed by such horns? We had come from a country of shy kangaroos fleeing with graceful bounds among other wild fleeing things. These were warlike animals quite capable of attacking without occasion.

Already the day passed and it was evening.

I stared at them as a person stares at death. I had become used to the free mix of wild species. Cattle were not part of that belonging, not even as food, being the Master's beasts. They could not mix with anything. Their portion was to continue eating the allotted grass and drinking at the allotted lagoon. Already their hoofs had pocked a deep trail down to the water, which I saw glimmering with sunset. The forest had been cut open for them. I recalled our arrival last year at a spot quite close to this: the Master and his servant on horseback, a sound of axes and crosscut saw, stripped logs floating beside the jetty. No doubt the timber was for sale, to be towed on a calm day to the nearest roadhead where hired bullock drays would cart them to a port from which they could be shipped to Sydney. In time there would be a bill of sale, a purse of coins. Such littleness, I thought. So much gone for so little return. The cutting of a forest I had once struggled through wounded me. My stomach dropped.

Thunder grumbled across the water, rolling in from the sea. Scuds of heavy cloud swept in. The cattle did not budge, but down at the lagoon two white horses looked up. By the tilt of their muzzles they were scenting the air. They began moving so graceful their hoofs scarce touched ground. Horses of mist. Ghost creatures from our fables. Hopes.

As the light began to die a slim figure emerged from the clump of bushes over to our left. Startled, she stopped. I could tell it was a girl, her supple movement and hesitating filled the emptiness inside me with joy. Not fifty yards off. She was caught facing us. In a manner of speaking she had fetched up against a sort of fence too—a fence no eye could see. She was one of the tribe, so already she expected what was to come.

Did the whir and whip of spears sound so entrancing to her? Her face still turned my way, her naked body pliant, she folded and fell.

The cattle, also intent on watching me, did not notice her fall.

Wild grief gripped my heart. I dared not run. But I had to know whether she breathed. Why should I care about my life if it cost her hers? Was I worth the two deaths the world had paid for me? I clamped a hand to my trembling mouth without even thinking it might mean something. Well, let the Men spear me too. Let them spear me in the back. I would never accept their offerings of food again. Either they could kill me quick or watch me waste away. Our chaste circle was broken by violence. Chain clucking, the iron bar thumped against my chest.

Until then I saw nothing strange. But that was when I realized something very strange had happened. An unearthly glow played about the heifers' heads, pale flickers, fitful prickles of white light dancing on the tips of their horns and wavering down the bone. When I say my hair stood on end, I believe it did. So some minutes passed before I knew that this was not the only reason why my head tingled. The light was on me too. I held still. I had seen St Elmo's fire only once before. But I had seen it and I knew what it was. I began shivering. For a moment more it darted around us, uncertain blue light, linking me with those dumb brutes, faltered and weakened. I felt it flare again as I turned to face the shadows (my guardians, my gaolers), to hold up my manacle and shake it at them, felt tiny thorns of light tremble on my hand while the metal came alive in my fingers.

There was no hurry now.

Under the gloom of baggy storm clouds, my sight further confused by a lens of tears, I strode through the grass to where the body lay. I fought to control my mad heart. I threw myself on my knees beside her and took her head in my hands—ordinary hands without meaning—a young man's hands—the hands of a lad who has known too little tenderness.

What I saw was that we were both young. She was a child from the women's camp, on the brink of being a woman herself. She might or might not have been beautiful, I don't know, but her youth was beautiful. Her slender arm, her smooth elbow, her cheek and long lashes. She lay on her side. My heart, so huge in me, filled my whole skin. The sight of her breast so tender and alive let loose a frenzy of grief. Both spears had found their mark: one pierced right through her neck, one dug deep in her belly. I sobbed dreadful convulsions. I had died and come back to find nothing changed. The old fears were waiting for me. I gave up with a howl of horror, such a long howl it left me fighting for breath. The voice blocked my throat. I struggled to draw the air I needed for life.

All this for this!

Alone, I was overwhelmed. Then came an answering scream. At first it seemed a thin sound, snaking up from the lagoon. The scream grew and swelled beyond human power. The shock of it cut like ice. I choked. I coughed out that solid plug of my own cry. I listened and listening gave me cold shudders. Returned to life, I squinted down that way, able to make out just enough. Pale forms plunged and bonded. The horses were mating. Spring had come.

At the time of my venture into the fine art of forgery I had been some years with a printer. We produced pamphlets, books bound in morocco, and everything between. I began by setting broadsheet ballads when I was fifteen, after four years an apprentice. Each broadsheet had a woodcut picture. As often as not I hawked the first batch in the streets of Douglas myself. They sold for a penny each. I was quite the young blade about town. But before long I was put on to more exact work.

My father thought the job a foible and not fit for a man to do. He said he expected I would grow out of it and take up something serious—perhaps in the line of his own work. My mother scolded him for a troublemaker. She encouraged me. As for Hall, my model in life, he brought us together by humouring our mother, following our father's trade, and singing the ballads I printed. His favourite would have you in stitches I am sure:

> Whack the folthe dah, dance to your partner
> Welt the flure yer trotters shake,
> Wasn't it the truth I told you,
> Lots of fun at Finnegan's wake.

That ballad, so filled with characters, was his favourite; not just for the tune, but because it sang the glory of getting drunk. In case you are wondering at his being christened Hall, his middle name was Henry, so both given names began with H. I thought this the grandest thing.

I was never drunk. Any time he led me on, Hall always kept a sharp eye on me. If I had had enough he invented some urgent call on our loyalty, a friend we must not let down, an appointment we must keep. I used to fret at this. I sulked a good deal, I dare say. I accused him of being selfish and maybe he was. But it is certain he loved me.

Your father is a man of trade, our mother said with a laugh and the wind dancing in among her hair, whereas you are a man of craft.

And what am I, then? cried Hall.

But she had no answer for him. Her eyes grew dark and her mouth helpless. Hall was her pet and she could not shame him.

I knew what was what, because she walked in her sleep.

Into the room we shared, many's the night I saw her creep and stop in the sightless way of her ailment, facing his bed but not looking down at him. If you ask me she sensed him through her skin. Then she would turn and wander back to the dreams of her own bed. Our father knew too, proof being that he was often awake when she returned cold, because a quarter hour later their bedhead started banging up against the wall.

Then began the nights when she stood in her sleep knowing Hall wasn't there. Those same nights she would find her sheets cold too when she made it back to bed, and wake like that. I lay fired with jealousy, jealous that she loved him best and jealous of his freedom to go out with our father. Hall could now claim to be in trade himself. Sundays they brought home quail eggs and a purse of earnings.

Trade is about the size of it, Hall told her with his eyes merry.

He lapped up the excitement and couldn't wait to put her through the torment again. This is the life of the people anyhow: either they go along with the law or they damn it to hell.

Does he have the skill, she asked her husband, notwithstanding that he talks too much? But she knew the answer already and turned to me. So you're the last hope of commonsense I am left, she said, and if you must go to the foolishness of making a fortune make it of the skill you have.

Welt the flure your trotters shake, sang Hall, wasn't it the truth I told you, lots of fun at Finnegan's wake.

He and I went out to trap some rabbits. As we tramped through the crunching heather I told him about her, how she walked in her sleep; I told him she stopped by his bed and that was all. We walked. He could be quiet when the time called for it. He laid an arm across my shoulders to show he understood. Then we played at wrestling. Unless on his part it was not play but the serious matter of proving that my worries on his account were uncalled for. With one arm he could withstand whatever weight I threw against him.

Taking string for the neat little trick we had with loops, plus a sack for the catch and several sticks, we came to the dragon stone.

A fanciful notion, Hall replied, setting me straight when I began to speak in a low tone of respect, a fish's body, a tiger's feet, a bat's wings and a tongue of fire. He laughed, scornful. Meat for some hero to kill before supper, he said.

This was what sent me to the shelf of books in the workshop. I knew one flaky leather spine bore the title, "Heroes in History and Fable". The first page told me that however important our history is to us our fairytales go deeper, that what we decide to do becomes history, but those actions going beyond choice fall into the pattern of the fables we are told. This book had a whole chapter from the Thebaid of Statius about two heroes, one called

Tydeus, but the other name slips my memory. Then came the commentary, just four pages long. Such a very suitable length.

I took my mother's advice.

I had not expected Oxford to be a deceitful town.

I came on foot, avoiding Derbyshire, home of the deposed King of Man, through Solihull and Warwick, Stratford upon Avon and Edge Hill, entering the county from the north-west. My last stop before Oxford was Banbury Cross. I mention Banbury, although the cross itself had long since been destroyed, because there, sleeping under a hedge, I had a dream. The sound of harps called my attention to a courtyard in which two persons rode round and round on horseback. The horses cantered in contrary directions, a young woman making the inner circle and a man in rich robes making the outer circle. They kept the same pace. But as they went round, the bridegroom grew in power until I looked for somewhere to hide, fearful that I might be caught prying. His raised arm a triumphant gesture, he threw back his head till what I saw of it was a bearded mouth. The beard jutted black with threads of grey. I remember this because I remarked—in the dream—how the myopic person's dreams are free of myopia. I am sure you are familiar with that fault in a dream when you go absent for a moment to dream you are aware of dreaming. During this lapse the horses had veered on to the same track. The emergency gave me a jolt, especially when I saw them merge to a single horse, a single rider—the mother—into whose body the lordly man disappeared. She caught me watching. She tugged at her jingling reins, turned the stallion's head, and came at me.

I never had this dream before. And never since. So I can be sure it was once only. I woke into the night, scrambled out. By broad moonlight I stumbled down on to the road and set off right away for Oxford. I would not risk another hour in that ill-omened spot. Twenty-two miles or no, I believed in my heart that if I did not reach my goal before the next night I never would. Such are the foolish fancies of the young who set themselves goals. I am amazed to think that it could not be more than three years since this happened, since a time when I would swear that if I arrived at some signpost before a bird flew across my path I would have seven years of happiness. You know the kind of thing? Well, this time I swore that unless I made it to Oxford I would never grow up. My idea of growing up, I might add, was to be like Hall.

The fields were freshly turned, apple trees were in bloom, and all the way a cuckoo called to me, always too far away to be seen. The land lay full of promise. And I got there, though we are talking about that time of spring when the nights still fall early. By dusk I came in view of the spires. I took a room in a public house because next morning I must present myself spruce for business.

As I say, I had not expected Oxford to be a deceitful town. I mistook its charm. The inn was a coach stage and across the yard a smith sat early in the day shoeing a post-horse amid the hubbub of arrivals and departures. He hammered nails with deliberation. He chose not to notice me when I went over and stood near. Having wished him good morrow and taken my place among some children who watched, I offered a comment on the quality of the beast. Tis her ladyship's own, he growled. The hammer blows made a sharp unpleasing sound. Metal on metal. Up until then I had not known how hungry I was but now an aroma of fried gammon filled the whole yard. I must not be tempted; I had so little money. I took my precious folio, promised myself a royal feast when I returned, and set out along backstreets behind the colleges.

At one point I asked my way of a young scholar not more than a year older than myself, thinking he must surely treat me kindly if for no other reason than the fellowship of youth. I took the route he pointed out, only to learn that he misled me so that I had to retrace my steps. Back where I started, and quarter of an hour wasted, I realized my purse had been stolen. There were four pennies in it, enough for a full meal of the best cooking, enough for goodness knows what else. Yet I must not be put off. I had the future and my family to think of.

I found the shops of three respectable dealers. Which would I try? Courage failed me because I admitted ignorance: not knowing what to look out for. I wandered from one to another and back, peering at them from across the street, pausing to pat a cur, gazing at reflections in a tobacconist's window to tell what I could, hurrying away, returning, loitering and then rushing past. I had not yet learned that timidity is the most dangerous vice or that such simple dodges would be noticed. It is likely I would be there still, growing long in the beard with dithering, but that, as I passed one for the fifth time and read yet again the gold-embossed sign, the wine merchant next door struck a cask with his mallet—the tuneful sound very different from horse-shoeing—I saw the spicket knocked out, the cask being mounted on a counter just inside the door. He began to fill a jug with dark frothing wine. I don't know why but that decided me. I called myself to order and took a deep breath.

The dealer, when he stood up from his desk to greet me, showed himself to be a tall man of sixty years or more. The veins of his hand were dark and particular as the rivers on the maps hung behind his desk. The smell of this place put me at home in an instant: leather and paper and old size. When I brought out my Commentary upon the Thebaid of Statius he treated it with reverence.

May I hold it? he asked, letting his eyes pop up to meet mine for a second only, and wheezing with greed. Yes, yes, he muttered, very . . . so very . . . might I look at it by daylight? . . . too kind . . . Thomas, Thomas, come this instant and open the door for me . . . the light is better in the back lane, my dear sir, where ivy on the walls softens . . . you don't mind? . . . shall treat it with perfect care . . . in all my years this is exceptional . . . found where do you say? the Isle of Man? an untapped source . . . most exceptional . . . the back door, Thomas, if you please, son . . . excuse me just a moment, I'll take my glass to look more close . . . need not insist on your coming with me . . . fetch a chair for the gentleman, Thomas . . . after you have opened the door . . . just one moment, sir.

This was the gist of it and the tone of his confidence. I have rehearsed the whole scene a thousand times since to convince myself how foolish I was not to see what he was at.

The dealer had scarce returned, bearing the vellum as if he had the Gospel there, written in Saint Mark's own hand, when Thomas set a bell dancing on its spring as he left us to our business. Already my heart was singing. But I was nervous in case I might not have the skill to strike a worthy bargain. What price would a professional man stick out for? You must see the problem yourself: how much was a unique handsel worth, a handsel printed by the father of printing, the master of us all?

You may not be aware, young man, that in the world of books one mystery outweighs all others, the dealer explained. We know it as the Old Hundredth . . . not the hymn, no . . . you might hear us say, the North Sea will go dry before we unearth the Old Hundredth . . . so-and-so will pay his debts when they find the Old Hundredth . . . this kind of jest. Let me explain. There are ninety-nine authentic publications from the Caxton press. One simply cannot conceive that the master would die content, in his seventieth year all said and done, without producing a hundredth. Even, perhaps, in his frail state not a full book . . . something brief and simple, but enough to bear his mark.

He bent his tall frame, stretched out his mapped hand, and pointed to the initials WC, a device I had laboured over.

The little bell danced again on its jingling spring. I did not look round. No doubt Thomas had returned. Of course I did not look round, my whole hopes were on my forgery. I willed my dealer to hurry up and name his price. He could have it cheap. He smiled.

There is no mistaking William Caxton's mark, he admitted, or this black-letter type . . . you don't find this in a modern printery. The qualmishness of his manner had gone, his hasty way of speaking gave way to a gentle summary. The only question left, he said, is how best to reward you for this priceless discovery . . . where was it found, do you say? in your family chest? . . . under the stairs? Remarkable!

A hand falling on my shoulder from behind made me jump. The constable flung his other arm around my throat and pinned me, sitting as I was, tight against him. His belt buckle cut into my ear. I cried out at the pain, comforted only that none of my kin could hear.

It amounted to this. A professor came to question me on my knowledge of the Manx language, which I was proud to prove I spoke. And then I was charged, as a foreigner in England, with theft of a national treasure.

Perhaps you do not need these things explained. Perhaps you know already or don't ever wish to know. Perhaps you can not be told but only made to feel. Whichever the case, you may think this letter comes from a disordered mind. So be it.

If I am putting the sublime and simple largeness of the whole at risk by focussing on yet more complications—supposing we mortals are capable of taking in the whole in the first place—you only need stand back a bit for these details to merge together, do you see?

So to the vexed matter of colonial prospects. The plan in many a good man's mind is to reach for great things, his vision being of broad pastures and himself raking in the plenty. He begins with a good run by ship from Portsmouth, landing sixty-nine days later at the Circular Wharf, enough pleasant company in the forward saloon to share his fantasy, with perhaps the surprise chance of the Governor's surgeon returning from furlough in Winchester on the same voyage and becoming so intimate as to promise he would press a friend's claim to a satisfactory offer of land. So we move along to the sighting of this land, a lovely cove, a cleft behind the dunes leading up to the belt of forest with the promise of natural grasslands beyond. Then the thrill of pacing the grant while deciding the spot for a house. The bush must be stripped and the timber sold in the next detail. But why go on? What is the point? You know this. And it can only be bitterness to me; denied even before I arrived. Let us not forget in what disgrace I came here and with what prospects of my own! But no, why should I flinch from listing the kitchen garden, the tomatoes and good potatoes? Even hardship and hazards may be welcomed, mayn't they—the torrential rain, the new road a frightful bog, all hands being called to drive a bullock team to the jetty with their freight of logs and then called to curb some skittish horses bolting for freedom (I see it all), the dray stuck on the slope and another squall sweeping in from the sea. Let us end the list with quiet satisfactions of an evening, lamps being lighted and a fire dancing in the hearth. What could be more vulgar? A novel, perhaps? Yes, a novel to be scanned but not read, or a sampler to be worked while the master of the house scratches his head over his ledger. An empire has been begun, leading in the end to visits from a bishop, a woolclip of three hundred bales and, crowning glory of all, a return trip home. Isn't that his style, to stride along a London street as a wealthy colonial?

Am I cruel enough?

When such sense has been made of the chaos here, success will give you leave to pity those who fail in their attempt upon the same goal.

But what happens if again we draw back from the detail

and take more of the wild land into our view? A long stretch of coast? Are you with me? Your vision widens to reach a hamlet perched on the shore, an outpost of stone and shingles like any little English port (forgery), its church a smaller copy of the very church you were baptized in (forgery), the citizens on the street respectable in full skirts and frock coats (forgery). But spare a moment to see past the fashions, the fences and straight roads, to see marooned folk lost and longing for the comfort of their bosky county home and hedgerows and Sunday rambles, cursing the Indians who fail to live up to Man Friday's example. Is this order? Will it be seen as such by an order-loving Maker?

For the moment I leave these questions with you.

Draw farther back. More wild hinterland. A longer stretch of coast dotted with more hamlets. But what if you have to compass this whole sea? And the next too? What if you must take in China on your right and the Cape Colony on your left? Can it be said that the sense you make of such chaos is other than a way of avoiding the whole? Does it make any sense at all when the scale is so large? Do you achieve more than a small voice in the enormous dark, a voice pleading: Lord let me know mine end, and the number of my days?

Meanwhile, what of the chaos? Don't it go its sweet way as chaos still?

I ask such questions because—at the end of my wanders in the circle of tree Men and bird Men—I could make nothing of the fence. An old dream had turned solid around me to hold me in its spell. I would never wake up. But this fright was nothing beside my anguish when I did recognize the fence and I knew I was awake. It brought back the smell of prison, the smart of shame. I knew then that we had not seen the worst of it. The most heartless violence would follow if settlers such as the Master ever lost their fear of the place and its people: telling one another they had come to a primitive land possessed only by a childlike race and that such simpletons, furnished only with accidental food, could be saved and civilized, brought to God, and that it would be a mercy to rescue them from the doomed calm of their backward ways.

Then, as if to prove me a hypocrite, there lay the corpse of a girl, and myself broken with grief. To me she was innocent. But to her own people she was not. Right until that moment I could be proud of having fitted myself into their world.

That night I heard ceremonies and wondered if the dead girl had a family, or if all children were children of the clan. I listened, choked by guilt. But for me she would be alive still. Again I saw the sprightly way she had stepped from behind the rock, her sudden halt, her shock, how astonished she was.

But isn't the notion of an accident just another detail in the fraud of order? Given a state of chaos, can there be accidents? Wasn't it by accepting life as whole, as beyond progress, that the Men had no need to sit in judgement of her? Instantly they knew what must be done. I overheard no discussion. So great is their knowledge that a mere detail can not distract them. The fact was enough. Nor did they have room for the superstition that she might be an instrument of spirit forces, a sacrifice to the greater good. She stepped on to the scene as part of the scene and remained as much part of it with spears deep in her neck and her belly. I did not need to draw back from the moment to see this. I took the moment in my arms because the risk I ran was also part of the chaos and true to it. I cradled her head in my hands. Her black hair hung warm and silky between my fingers. Dust smudged her cheek. The last light of day sparkled in one eye.

So I saw the bird Yllerion. There in the eye of this unknown lass, a wing as sharp as a razor, the fiery point of a feather plunged into the sea. Ordinary birds swept around us, drawn to the fall by a high wind. Of course, according to the book from which I made my forgery, Yllerion will rise again. I know that.

If you are to understand how I came to commit murder I must face the pain of setting down the sick man's last try at humour. Can you picture us, the convicts, chained in pairs but otherwise slumped as we pleased under the fitful puddle of light given out by a swaying lantern. Gabriel Dean was by then so ill that each sally at my expense cost him half an hour recovering. But he had won his point: one sarcastic word from him and those sixteen toadies obliged by sniggering.

This fellow here is called Suck-prick, or Shit-nose, he said, driving himself up on to the prop of an elbow to introduce me around, and collecting his energy in bursts.

Sniggers.

We shall leave Suck-prick for a better time; but why he is called Shit-nose is because his job will be to clean up my shit.

Laughter. Bones cracked in my shoulder as he forced my hand to where he sat and underneath his stinking pants.

Clean it all out, he growled hoarse. I'm a particular man.

Sniggers, also a single: Pieuw!

He sighed and let me go. You can eat it if you like, he offered.

That night I watched the lantern gutter—the oil had run dry. My misery stretched minutes out to hours. In these hours futile ideas churned in my brain. Then came a thought to stand like a bright presence among the dross. Everybody else slept. Soon the lamp would go out, its little tongue of flame dry and dying to a red ember. The wick smouldered. Meanwhile my tormentor rolled from side to side, slippery with sweat, strength drained from his boneless meat, the fever at its height. By morning, if he lived, he might be over the worst. And that was likely, his constitution being what it was. He would be ready to take up the new life awaiting us.

My idea stood so bright among the dross it bewitched me with its beauty: the only weapon I can use in my defence is myself.

I took scrupulous note of how he lay; also the exact position of his head. Each time he rocked or shifted I printed his new position in my memory. The hours crept on. Maybe they lasted half the night, I have no way of knowing. Then the tiny flame faltered, revived, flared up, and died to a glowing ember. The ember winked and went out. The dark in my skull burst as dazzling snowflakes. I listened for any footfall. The ship creaked a lullaby. Beasts shuffled sleepless below. I thought of Noah's wife and Noah, the sneaky way God played favourites to take the rest of mankind by surprise. I thought of home and the last war and Wellington's victory. I thought of the tale we were told of a French prisoner spitting in a British officer's face: I would be justified, the British officer said, if I put a musket ball through your head, but I shall not give myself the pleasure because I wish to show that I know better how to behave than you; I will add, however, that it is lucky you spat at me and not at one of my subordinates. Preachers went all round the Isle of Man repeating that. It may not be so lucky for those among you who reject Jesus Christ that you spit on me.

I raised myself to my knees. The silence itself seemed aware of my risky plan. I had to keep the manacled hand quite still on the floor, not to jerk his end of it.

Gabriel Dean's breath came shallow and fast.

Now, with the greatest care, I moved my locked arm, easing his as well, to give me room to twist round. I listened.

He did not respond. By the faint sucking sound I think he still rocked a little. I could smell his slather of sweat.

I believed. At that moment I believed in a forgiving God. The end of all flesh is come before me, He whispered, for the earth is filled with violence.

The weapon, as I say, was to be my body. I calculated its most effective weight to be at the solar plexus, which was also pliant. I did not throw myself upon him. Quite otherwise. From the kneeling position I leaned over, taking my weight on the free hand, intent on remembering the precise whereabout of his face, then lowered myself, very gentle, until I felt his nose touch me at the base of my chest. I shifted position an inch or two. Then pressed firmly down.

The turmoil of thoughts was gone: my mind empty and peaceful. His body thrashed in its coma. But his fever was my ally. We bucked together. Why had I not expected these horrifying jolts? From ignorance of what I was to do, you see. We pounded away with dull padded thumps. The other convicts woke: I could hear their unasked questions. The bucking grew more violent.

Please! I cried out in pain. Oh please, no!

They lay listening to us thudding on the planks. Dean's free arm flopped and beat at me. I gripped his head to hold it tight under me so that even when he lifted me by the power of his neck he could not free his nose and mouth. The pad I had made of my tunic held in place. I kept my midriff slack as I could. But the struggle went on too long. How could he live without air?

Help! I gasped with real desperation.

Certain that every one of them must now be awake, my hatred for them grew beyond any pain I might have felt at their betrayal. They knew I was being murdered. There were enough of them to save me. Yet not one uttered a word. The cowards lay, each man in an agony of waiting, until the difficulty was finished with.

But it did not finish. Spasms kept humping up against my flesh, eruptions and shudders. His body twisted, bridged. This bridging was the first sign of a stratagem. I was no longer suffocating an unconscious victim. If he got one breath of air he would get others. I knew I was failing. Even with his illness to help me I could not resist him. I saw flashes of red light in my head (that is what I remember now) while stabs of fire ran about my body, sharp in the blood, raking at the small of my back and my shoulders.

Help! I let out a yell of panic.

But the bridge had already collapsed. Gabriel Dean slumped under me and lolled as if his backbone were snapped. My tunic sopped up our sweat. I grew aware of myself, sprawled, one arm twisted against his at a painful angle, in agony from the iron bearing across my forearm.

Somebody let out a discreet play-actor's snore.

"Fraternity" creaked about her lazy business. Rat claws snickered across the deck to visit this possible meal then that. Could murder be smelt already? I slapped with my free hand to protect Gabriel Dean's handsome person from being gnawed at and began to free my shackled arm. I put my ear to his chest, surprised by the feel of springy hairs crackling against the side of my face. I could hear no heart beat. He lay dead, limp and invisible.

As I say—they let me cradle the girl's head in my hands and feel her warm hair among my fingers. Nobody speared me for it.

I had been asleep a long while when I woke to a disturbance, a steady spitting crackling noise. The world was still dark as the grave. Dazed, I wondered where I was, with a king's pennants flying in the wind, breaking to sparks and swirling past me down the hill. Points of fire winked across the night sky and left a cut of smoke in my nostrils. I sat up, fuddled and exhausted. From the ridge, back there where we had slept the previous night, little bobbing flames snaked in line. From the other direction, down by the bay, clusters of them gathered and crept across the sand dune. Beyond, wavering among forest trees to the north, yet more specks of fire arrived to converge with the others. Standing at my vantage point beside the fence I watched, enthralled. I wished then for sharper vision because the prettiness of this scene was beyond fancying. The customary million insects trilled and chirruped. An owl screeched from a distance, the same owl had tracked us the whole way from the mountains, I was sure of his hollow ominous note. Otherwise all was hushed.

My protector and my guardians, whom I now swore to disown, were nowhere to be felt, not even at their established distance. By habit I was used to sensing their body heat, but now the air had gone cold. Just when I began to master the lack of being private, I was dropped into privacy deep as the ocean. This was not the aloneness of a Byzantine emperor, untouchable as the god he was supposed to be: I had been left where I lay, as a thing no longer any use.

By going to the murdered girl I broke the contract of my sanctuary, you see. During the many months of this sanctuary, layer after layer of aloneness peeling away, I had learned to live with what was left. Yet now, a total and naked solitary, I felt my lack of defences as a kind of security. I don't know how to put the point but, after the grief of holding that dead girl, I might have expected anything other than this.

Then excitement clawed at my whole being. A burden lifted from me, my spirit leapt with freedom. To accept was enough. Why should anything be thought about? I knew. And I knew the whole sensation of knowing as the blood pounded and set my head spinning. I soaked up the glory. There was a fresh warmth in the air, scented with woodsmoke and sea-drift.

The truth came on me, sudden as being taken up by an eagle: those flames flickering down there were justice for my wrongs.

Who is to call vengeance base? Or lust either? Do they not bring us to our most glorious flights? Clanspeople who had never seen me were settling my account. Yes, because I knew what that hollow held where they gathered. No sooner had I welcomed this than my excitement soured, the underbelly of revenge being guilt. This was proof that I had not yet acquitted myself of my crime against Gabriel Dean. Nor my passive crime against the girl. Not far under the guilt I discovered fury. Fury at the savage way I was punished for my original misdeed—that test to put my talent at full stretch—for attempting to defraud those who exploit us all the time and sit in tyranny over our island people. Fury against myself for speaking so feeble at my trial too. Many's the time on the voyage to Sydney I had practised the sort of eloquence I hoped to rise to, denying English law altogether, proud of being a prisoner of war, challenging the Earl of Derby to appear in the witness box and answer my charges, ending on a climax of damning the English for the mortal injustice of my father's execution.

If this was vengeance, then I lusted for it.

When I thought of my darling mother and her woe, my rage burned fiercely. I thought of Hall and his unknown fate, so gallant in following our father's profession. Hall, when refusing to let me take the same risks, unwitting that he thrust me into a more and more fixed determination to be our mother's hero, to outwit the enemy over there on their home soil through their vice of coveting things. To hell with it: how was I to know Caxton published ninety-nine volumes? I chose Caxton only because I had not heard of anyone else!

I was telling you, I think, that our house at Kirk Braddon stood half a mile in from the sea. Some similarity in situation here on this foreign soil damped the bright thought of flames. With no moon yet, the sea glimmered dully out there. Certain it is that I thought of home and the marauders of old burning down our monastery. Had I become a marauder myself?

Picture me: my scabby insect skin, stick limbs, and leaf veins down the inner side of thighs and forearms, rags of a faded blue shirt buttoned round my neck, the whole caked in a chrysalis of clay. I was what the Men wished me to become. I was, if it came to the point, what my persecutors also wished me to become, supposing they could ever conjure such a scarecrow.

The sheer number of flames appalled me. Whose hopes were burning?

Out to sea lowering clouds grumbled, the threatened rain held off as it did the evening before, when I had been touched by St Elmo. Meanwhile, across to my left a swift carpet of fire passed across the flat. The best I could make out otherwise was a chrysanthemum of glittering gold, which must surely be a bonfire or a whole building going up. Fine drifts of moisture being carried on the wind wafted down as a mockery.

I took my decision. Tying the knife to my waist with a shred of shirt sleeve, clutching the talisman of my manacle and stepping firm, I ducked through the fence where the cattle were kept and down a slope. No one emerged from the night to stop me. I could see quite well enough by the light from a screened moon. Reaching the lagoon, I came out from the fence and stepped on to the road.

You may not think stepping on a road could mean much. Well, nor did I. My feelings took me wholly by surprise. A long time had passed since I felt a road underfoot. It spoke to me by righting my stance. I had been out of touch. I had not even seen my own face since I grew beyond age. With no friend to help me escape, by mercy of a shot or a dagger in the back, I had become lost to myself. The chap I used to know was last seen stepping over the gunwale of a boat and wading thigh-deep at the edge of the ocean; the chap I used to know was a heart in a painful basket. Under the weight of that stormy night my relics walked, bones clicking into place as I passed along the road, on my way back to strike a blow, to win my brother's respect, to send a message home, to cry, Down with the King!

Several times I suspected that shadows were keeping pace with me on the far side of the fence, but could never be sure. Though I remembered some buildings from last time I was not prepared for the cluster I saw ahead, almost a village, where the livestock was already in full cry. Chickens raced, shrieking and night-blind, for their hutches. Two dogs jerked at chains, thrown into collision by the same frenzy, gashing one another as they bounced apart, to be tripped by their bonds and tumbled in the dirt as furry bundles.

Several gunshots went off: brisk and to the point.

A horse reared at the garden gate, striking the rail with a rapid thudding like the kettledrums people used to beat in the wake of the dead while winding along the streets of Douglas following an open coffin with someone inside. Again and again the horse reared up to pound the solid timber. Hundreds of wordless flares were carried dancing across the compound, eddying among the buildings. Unseen men shouted from inside and a scream flew loose above the shouts. I ran that way. And once I ran I knew for certain that my guardians ran as shadows, keeping pace with me.

Bastards! I wailed at the same time as my heart sang to see a shed go up, flames catching the bark roof. The catastrophe came so quick there could be no stopping it. Glory! I whimpered when the roof curled in a single contraction and tore loose from the frame put there to clamp it down. A rampage of heat punched my body, knocking the breath out of me. Whose idea was this fire? And why? The Men could have no motive of their own: how had they been injured? Beyond this small parcel of land, our journeys through their country had never brought us to any other invasion by settlement. The only evidence of any stranger intruding on the dense disorder had been those few leavings we found, such as my knife. Not enough. No.

The truth was this, that while the Men knew no word of my language they must have known my thoughts. So, they had felt my fury and sensed my need. They had obeyed. I had given orders as sure as if I spoke them. Who knows whether rage shows in subtle colours on the skin to those with skill to see, as holiness glows about the heads of saints? They were innocent of blame. Thus I could point to no other culprit than my own anger. I was the one who willed this. In my divided and deceitful heart I demanded it, lusted for it.

The shed burned. The strong flames roared. The dogs fell silent in a heap.

Caught in the middle, where did I belong? I had long known I was like to be torn between great forces, but would not let such a thing happen. Until that moment I had kept myself from the real pain.

It does matter, after all, how we die. Between death and near-death I must put my proof to the test. Must I confess, then, that my enemies and I came of the same mould? Was my unjust sentence no more to be abhorred than an unjust acquittal? Was it all one, in the end, when face to face with this other thing, this pure chaos, this world free of categories, of individual choice or moral dispute? The joy I found in revenge, by the time it broke over me, was becoming a wave of shame. What had I led my guardians into? What fury of an eye for an eye might follow their victory? The redcoat garrison in Sydney hungers for just such an invitation to perfect their bloodthirsty skills.

A lick of flame shot up the side of the house itself while I watched. I do not know what noises I let out. By the time I came to myself I was gagging my mouth to stop a howl that seemed to have gone on longer than the lost air of my lungs. I crept near. A dark block of roof stood in silhouette against the steady glare from some fires behind. A house. The word stood up with the thing itself, its meaning solid as walls and as much at risk.

Do you see my dilemma now?

Shouting with joy at the Master's fall, I felt the ground shift under me. Was there ever a time in my childhood before I knew what a house was: the pitched roof, four walls, square windows, smoke which was supposed to spout from the chimney only?

I whooped encouragements. Yet I was like a ship whose hull sweeps on by its own thrust, well after the captain's command to heave-to is clear and the rudder has already been thrown hard over. Leaping out of the night, Men set torches to whatever would burn, raced away as far as the gully, and raced back up on the unseen side. Meanwhile this wonderful idea, this house, the uses of confining space and closing it in, whispered an irresistible call to my loyalty. The idea of a house was my inheritance which, however I might be convicted, could not be taken from me.

A rush of intense heat engulfed the timbers. The building fluttered feathers from between its rough cut slabs. Dazzling claws dug into the doorposts. I could admire how solid the frame was put up. Right across the roof the shingles were outlined with fluid gold. The making could never have been so beautiful as the destroying of it. The swarm of torches spilled like red mercury, forming a pool and then running out on a sudden, trickling too fast and unpredictable for a man to catch, a few beads broken loose joining together to dart out of an opening, only to circle as the land tilted, tricky, slippery. Voices chanted and flickered about me. A thousand black birds broke free and flew in all directions from the explosion of fire. The roof, bulging and wavering, shone like a live flank of scales; while from the end of the house a broad wing lifted, a wing large as a tree, lit along its edge by loss and ruin.

You will want to know if I saw any survivors after hearing those several shots.

Forgive me. The horror fresh in my head, I must put down my pen. Night is come. Darkness seeps in to swallow me. I shall answer you. I shall find the strength to answer tomorrow. For now I am lost and faint with confusion.

This morning I woke before dawn, thinking of what I wrote last night. How I came to shed tears I cannot now explain—unless because a burning house suggests the frailty of our strongholds. Was it grief for the Master and his hopes? Or for myself and mine?

A shaft of pink light has just fallen across the page. I am laughing because my nose almost touches it—such is the effort I must make to see what I am putting down. Impatient to have you read what I tell you, fear torments me in case my frankness offends. I begin to understand more about my untested needs.

I fret at having to suffer being shut away again and left here, this latest indignity, yet I shall never believe you are to blame. You could not be so cold. Meanwhile, I shall push on with the task. There is still much to be set down.

Let me take you back again to the fire. I mentioned several gunshots. Well, the house was already lost by then, I suppose. A door swung open and a figure stood there. Are we not used to seeing the past look out from a gilded frame, plump and self-satisfied, dressed in a Sunday waistcoat buttoned right to the top, beside a spouse in her Sunday bonnet? This, then, was the nightmare counterfeit of the same picture, the spouse being gone. It was, perhaps, the future which I saw in that gilded frame. And what a future, dazed by facing disaster, while tucking a flintlock under one armpit to tap more powder into the pan! As if shooting into the colossal night had not been futile enough, the fellow cocked his piece and made ready to fire again. The light being so hot and brilliant about him, surely he was too blinded to make out those shadowy forest spirits and their agile leaping? Yet he took aim and let fly. There was a wink of red fire. The sound of the shot could scarce be made out this time, such was the general din of popping and booming. Then, quite near me, one of the Men fell, even as he was running past. His fire stick rolled right to my feet. At close range I could now see that the stick itself did not burn: a thick bulb of resin sizzled like tar. The fumes threw me into a fit of coughing. I doubled up. I was still coughing and in a seizure when the next shot hissed past my head to rattle among shrubs at my back.

I hobbled away from the light of the torch, still in a hacking fit, to stumble among foreign shadows. I fell. I crawled.

Brilliant as sunrise the buildings burned. Winds whirlpooled from all directions, drawn towards the inferno.

Only at this desperate last minute did figures come dashing out. Impossible to tell how many, perhaps ten, perhaps more, racing clear of the collapsed roof. They dodged haphazard—and this was their downfall, because they collided with one another and fought. So it took a while for me to realize the spearings had begun. By that stage I knew myself for a traitor already and one who let this happen. You see, I did not come between them and their killers, although I believe my power was such that I might have stopped the butchery just by holding up my manacle, evidence of my disgrace.

What I want you to understand is that I did not notice the spears in time because my mind was absorbed by another task: to seek among those darting outlines for glimpse of a skirt. All my energy and powers were bent on the single moment when I would be most needed. I knew there was a woman around the place and I reserved my courage for her. The men did not matter. If they could not look after themselves, they must wait the worst. But I declined to watch her murdered the way the natives had already murdered a young woman of their own. I had no room for more than one pitiful memory of a pierced throat. And yet—and yet—the more I work here at this task and strive to explain myself to you, the more I suspect I am winning battles against my own truth. Each sentence I set down shuts me farther away behind a barricade of tidy excuses.

I confess I do not know why I did (or did not do) anything.

The best I can say is that I did not leap in among those frantic figures. I did not shake my manacle with terrible majesty. Nor waste an instant debating the case against myself. Nor indulge my grief or guilt. I watched. And took no part. I crouched. And saw pouncing forms, cowering forms. Torches snaked and fluttered among ruins, shedding sparks and puffs of smoke thick as clubs. The attackers sped from shadow to tactical shadow; they struck and struck.

The livestock panicked. I felt the delicate thrill underfoot as their bulky mass went pounding this way and that inside the fence. Voiceless and desperate they lumbered off—I heard them gasp and wheeze—only to come lunging back through the night a minute or two later, pumping at the terrible bellows of their despair. Huddled against the fence as I was, all I could see of them were fleeting glints of fire in their eyes or the glow picked on the point of a horn. All I could feel was that shudder of earth and the passing puff of damp breath. Meanwhile, high in the valley a vague cloud of sheep drifted across the hillside, compacted, broke apart and drifted again. The horse which screamed kept screaming.

Ash rushed up the funnel of flames, loosed from the bondage of weight. Months of labour, in the form of beams and rafters, swirled beyond reach. Space claimed them. They were gas, they were a spiral of light, they were the origin of a new star. While, answering that roar of loss, came the willynilly thunders from the storm just out to sea.

Still no shape of a woman ran clear, though by now it was already too late and the attackers cast away their torches, setting fire to crops.

From beyond the cup of firelight, when the noise began

to lessen, the funeral pounding of the ocean could be heard again along the beach. Waves could also be heard to joggle a barbarous instrument of timbers. Floating logs clocked and bumped in restless collision.

Tell me, are we in 1838 yet? I feel old enough. I am in my twenty-first year at any rate.

A tragedy sloughs off useless details and this includes time. The thing exists itself, with any rough corners knocked away and smoothed by handling. The frenzy is distilled as one clear simple scene, another clear simple scene, and another. Not that such scenes are tranquil even if we see them as still. They are charged with energy so pure it may inspire a man to heroic risks. I saw this and felt it. I saw a shadow wearing a hat, he stooped double to hurry out from the blazing barn, he was in the act of rolling something across the yard. He kicked at it. I wondered if this might be a large ball. Or a biscuit barrel, perhaps? Having sent it rolling and bouncing down the slope toward the house he stood up, a perfect target, and removed his hat to give a theatrical salute.

In the next scene the hat was tucked under one arm while spears flickered round him—some thonging the air, others stuck trembling in the ground—and an immense burst of light responded to his salute. The battleground was revealed: a few staggering defenders and an awed bunch of attackers, corpses at different stages of grasping the earth, chickens dashing zigzag from calamity to calamity.

When the blast of it hit me I heard my skull crack.

I picked myself up and all I could think was that I had lost my knife. I had to search for it on all fours. Why had I never used that knife? I condemned myself. If I had only thought of a use for it I might have staved off this conflict. Such was the childish way I thought. (Now, much later, I might defend myself by arguing that I could not be held responsible for what others did: neither the Master with his ambition nor the Men who wanted their land back.) After the explosion I shrank from new flashes of light, only to realize they were nothing more than the arriving storm.

So the settlement burned. The business of flames tackled this section then that. Once the living quarters were gutted a satisfactory start was made on the kitchen. Dark coils of shadow spent themselves. Is this what I wanted, I asked, a triumph of ruins? You already know about my habit of guilt. Well, the disaster was so tremendous and I wept so savage that I was brought to the point of groping for the blade. What else did I deserve but to fall on it? Wasn't I one of the Men, the very centre of their circle? Hadn't I let them use me as a mascot for their courage, proof that the invaders were not spirits after all? Didn't I, all unwitting, act as the medium for working magic? Such matters can never be known for certain, but what was sure was that my protector often went unarmed, yet I had made no attempt to go for him with my knife, and after all I am a man who knows how to plan a murder, even with an inadequate weapon.

I felt curiously like the eunuch in some pasha's palace, the harmless witness brushed aside by great events, known to the powerful on both sides but in each case let go as being of no account.

Ash and glowing debris sailed higher and higher. I crept through the fitful dark, the night itself seeming to flicker and fluctuate, hands groping as I went. The soil smelled good, already swarming as it was with alarmed beetles and centipedes. I jabbed my knee on a flint. The mingled violence of fires sounded more than ever like babbling voices, arguments and singing. I peered around but the place stood deserted. A lone chicken went belting across the yard and straight into the oven of a crumbling out-house. The fires crackled companionable together.

The Men were gone.

As a scene, this had the fancifulest beauty. Throat dry, I watched a family's hopes being eaten away by cankers of night, gobbled into that black mass bloating and swooping above the hail of ash. I do not believe I had given much thought to ideals for some time and the notion struck me as full of tricks: such a frail ideal as a new life or a new society will remain forever beyond reach. And the ideal of a farm carved in virgin territory is not far different from the ideal of justice in a court of law. Each one being suited to the fool who falls for it. I found my knife and kept hold of that. The knife would be enough salvation for me.

Excuse my clumsiness, but the blots are not entirely of my making. Your nibs are cheap things, a brand we would never use at the printery, not even for writing invoices.

Is this new one better?

I know where I left off: that dark wing as big as a tree and a roof being the dragon's wavy flank. Well, such dragons breathe pestilence too. Whatever burned with a foul reek burned amid the last sumptuous climax of fire. A gold pyramid sank and slumped and cataracted down as scattered jewels, while flurried plumes bunched and fluffed to soar away as whirling stars and popping blossoms of light, and the black wind scurried among stark statues of lightning—all suddenly netted in delicate silver ghostliness. Drifting every way at once, a glitter of air sealed the burnt-out posts and frames in glass. Falling falling falling. Timeless, unhurried, ever new, delicate among raging flames, falling from rolling upside-down hills, fragrant as the fresh sea: rain. Rain, bright with the prism of an insect wing, folded wavering vanes over the ravaged land. The parapets of bonfires burned more energetic. I witnessed the sky as a spinning muddle of lights that stung the eyeball and rested on the lashes with glints of chance green, chance violet, chance orange. Thunder wallowed around while the rain set in until the whoosh of the fire dulled. High along the ridge beyond the sheep paddock, one lick of flame poked right to the verge of the forest and then died.

While tying my knife into my rags again, the thought visited me that I had just watched weapons of war employed with the cunning of Napoleon—fire and water. The downpour moved inland in the wake of destruction, drenching a softer darkness where it fell, to reach right up among the wild hills.

Is the mastery of fire what makes us human? Is this the one thing denied the rest of the animal kingdom? I am reminded of the dragon, his swimmer's body, his walker's armaments, his flyer's swiftness, each one possible for other creatures. The mystery being his tongue of fire.

Yet, when you think of the individual human beast, who among us could manage fire without help? What a tyrannical master it would be! Just to keep the fire alight through all seasons, with never a day's holiday, never an hour, or it would be out and lost. Whole families must have dedicated themselves to a single fire. Whole tribes, as I see it, had to come together and stay together for that one thing only. They had to learn to manage fire. But where tribes in most countries settled to this task and nursed their gift in some sheltered spot known for safety, until they began building special shelters for it (you see how I work?), in this country Men dared a risk more skilful. Like jugglers they have found a way to keep it with them wherever they wander. The tribes of Britain or the Isle of Man settled down, having to be content with the same place every day for a thousand years, where these Indians are free to move and have always been free to move because they care nothing for any possession other than this one thing—they dedicate their lives to the miracle of carrying it with them, asleep in the sticks they rub together (I have seen it done), asleep in the dry foliage they pile up, asleep in their own breath, for all I know, with which they blow the smouldering leaves to life.

Think of the Library of Alexandria going up in smoke. What power did the printed word have then?

The blaze subsided. Oblivion rained on charred structures and on the earth. The occasional still-burning timber, eaten out by night worms, glared a moment and fell, kicking up a wreckage of sparks which were soon doused. The grey smudge across the landscape was as much steam, I suppose, as smoke.

My heart cried out. I stood up and rushed to see if there was anybody left to be helped. Lightning still strayed out along the horizon but it was not much use to me; in the main I saw by the sullen glow of the ruin itself. Groping across a slick of fresh mud, I peered into the victims' faces and felt for their hearts. Five dead. Six. All dead. I expected to recognize them. I plied my brains to match a nose or hairline with some memory, overwhelmed by my longing to be known—even by a corpse. If these were total strangers to me, so was I to them. Helpless. Frustration drove me on. I think I began shouting. All I asked was to rescue someone's name or voice, not even anything you could touch, from my days in Hell. Then I began doubting even such memories as I had. Soon the only ghost I could call up before my anger and put in the dock was Gabriel Dean. His face became every man's face. His voice, his smell, his sneer. I scrambled away. And tripped over another body. This one's hat, having fallen to one side of him, lay turned up to catch the rain. The light was so poor I had to put my face right close to his to see who it was.

The Master.

I felt no pity for him. My own needs were too demanding. Instead what hit me was gratitude. The enormity of this gratitude choked me and left me dumb. I laid my subtle hand, the doubter and compromiser, against his cheek. How could I thank him for being there, dead though he was, for reminding me who I had been? At last I knew what it was to give away the life of a god and be willing to embrace our shoddy human fate. Injustice too, yes, I embraced that as well. Yet I was not about to become victim of another ritual; if he was the first bridegroom, he could remain the only one. My voice did sound at last while more rain pelted down, whipping round me in gusts.

Why you? I croaked, as I remember.

The sound came guttural with lack of use. All around us, in the storm, the shell of his plan for the future glimmered. Beyond the shell, across blackened pastures, that miraculous cloud of sheep passed again, still clustering dispersing and regrouping.

Only then did a brief flare up of flame shine on the fallen man's open eye, bright as the back of a teaspoon, a watching eye, and I realized it was him growling: Bleeding traitor—I'll hang you for this!

I sprang back. He must have been in fearful pain, spears still stuck out of him. Yet he lunged at me. He grabbed my ankle, then my wrist. He held me.

I'll hang you, he whispered again as if the whole affair had already turned into a victory.

I wrenched myself free. But he caught the manacle and hitched the chain round his own wrist. Must I murder him as I murdered Gabriel Dean?

You heathen, his voice grew strong.

I knew him for certain. What was I to do? Was I to pull out one of the spears, though sick with death, and use it a second time? I could not rise to the deed again. I threw myself back. He hung on like a lunatic. I already understood what it was to be shackled to another man—and he did not. That was the difference. I drove my fist at his face. He astonished me by twisting aside and ripping my knife from the bindings I had made for it. My own knife. He stabbed at me, gashing my shoulder open, then slicing a flap of flesh under my good arm, then aiming for my head with a swing that lifted his trunk clear off the ground. Between each thrust I punched his face. I dragged him to one side as I threw myself back. We slithered in the mire with the terrible effort. I was sobbing. My knife was gone. He jerked at the manacle until the string made from my hair worked loose and flopped about, growing longer as we fought. Those lost hairs had been the only measure of my time among Men. Years of hair. My ritual observance was to keep what could not be had again. My sufferings were coming loose and being thrown away. Such loss could never be replaced. While I wasted a moment trying to stuff the long end back, the blade snicked my thigh. The Master grunted. The hair string, itself bonded with clay, fell apart and more slipped out. I could not stop it. Again the Master raised his trunk, dragging at me so that I strained to bear the weight of him. I tumbled back into the slime and rolled down the slope. My bones knew what my exhaustion had no mind for catching up with: I was free.

So thin had I become that once the hair packing was gone the manacle slipped off my wrist.

My bones propped me on my feet and set me staggering away along the road. There my mind caught up. I knew the truth. My mind took over and directed my drunken totterings as if now the bones had grown soft. I drove myself. I had to get away. I would survive in the wild. He could not follow. So I turned my back to the fire and made what haste I could. Stopping on the road only once to catch my breath I wavered there. At that moment a figure loomed out of the night to come right upon me, flapping queerly, heading in the opposite direction. I dodged aside. My ankles gave and I collapsed. I picked myself up and faced death. But the figure had gone. Slipping and grovelling, I made my escape. The storm crashed over me. Repeated stands of lightning now lit the country as a sequence of pictures. Sea thundered along the sand. My blood pulsed with its own thunder. I did not look back. The last of my blue rags having been ripped off me with the knife, my sores stinging like hornets, I fled up along the boundary of the paddock to where fence timbers hung smashed from the posts. A piece of splintered rail pierced my foot.

The cattle were out.

I reached the spot at which earlier that evening—a century earlier—I had wept for a young girl and believed no worse horror possible. I did not stay. I pressed on, gasping for strength to reach the trees where I last saw my guardians stand still as sticks and calm . . . though I knew that on the ground beside each man lay a spear, held between two toes, ready to be flipped up into the hand.

I detest what I have become. You bring out the worst in me. Day after day I labour to recover the truth. I was all right before—I could abide my faults. But now I come to the point of seeing myself as a dupe and an idiot.

Why should I not be loyal to my parents and my homeland? Then again, supposing all trade is trickery in some degree (which I swear it is), why am I suddenly worse than another and fit for the hangman? Ought I to be afraid of saying I hate your England simply because I suppose you are English?

Well, I do not care to have sympathy on those terms. As for the wrong I am thought to have done respectable persons, let me say that the most respectable have been brutal enough to me—from the lackeys of Derby to the mealy-mouth gentry of the courtroom. If I am to offer you anything, let me offer myself whole, heady with anger and despising those who persecute me.

As to my reason for writing at all, this must be clear by now. You are my hope. I think of you the entire time. I wait for you. I listen for you. I ask: Have you no heart? I curse you and then my eyes fill with tears and I turn the curses against myself. I think of the future (of you on horseback, for some reason, at full canter, and I fear for your life). I think of the past (of you seated in lamplight staring at the hearth, startled by some presentiment and yet basking in comfort, unable to shake off the pleasures of ambition).

Then I think of you today, living in hunger and fear, and I say again: Come to me.

Let me show you my notion of perfect order. There it is, a tiny island. By kneeling on the English shore and reaching out you could take this island, cup it in your hand and lift it, dripping, from the sea. It is the world seen through a lens, details sharper than life, with a single specimen of each thing needed by a world: one good harbour, one mountain, one ring of standing stones, one earth fort from prehistoric times, one castle, one dragon.

To the north of the mountain lies a fertile plain, to its west a clean-swept stony ridge, to the east a wet vale where herds graze. To the south of the mountain lies a pocket of tropical palm trees planted by one of the Goddess's doomed bridegrooms who still carried her palm frond and her blackthorn in his hand and who stuck them in the ground together on his way to death in luxury.

The island stone is old, the river is old, the story of courage is old as the river. There has been time for everything. Order rules. Fields are ploughed in furrows straight as combs. Orchards are planted in rows. 1 2 3 4 5 6 has been called mathematics and carried right through to a zero for ten and two zeros for a hundred. Musicians take the trouble to tune their instruments. Nothing gets wasted in this little world. Even the sheep's back is clipped for wool. Not only are there laws but agreed ways of breaking laws. Legal ways of smuggling. And, among those who smuggle in a manner considered rude and blameworthy, there is humour. You see how perfect it is and how complete?

I am peering through my lens. I see miniature folk who build stone houses with slate floors and slate roofs. They live in families. They know nothing of the loneliness of chaos. Look close. Although you have had to reach your hand as far as it will go to take hold of this island, every leaf and whisker is perfect. So soon the gorse dries out on the hills. Today is the day of the Melliah because a corn crop has been harvested from all but the last corner of the last field. And now the job will be finished. People laugh while they work with sickles. The farmer already sets up a keg of ale. Young wives arrive and set their infants down to sleep on shawls spread in the shade of a hedge. The heat is getting up. If you put your ear close you can hear this heat as bee wings humming. The older ladies make tea at a trestle table and pour buttermilk into cups for the children, who gallop through stubble and call for the feast to begin. The prettiest miss has the honour of reaping the final swath and she does it at a blow. Men mop their heads. They unbutton their waistcoats. Women loosen bodices and throw down tools. They gather at the table to be thanked by the farmer, who looks like my mother's old man and speaks directly to God to thank Him too. But look closer—even while he thanks his friends a lass comes running from the farmhouse, don't she? One clog slips off and her ankle turns in the ditch. She reaches for his shoulder. She hangs her weight on his shoulder. At first he can not make sense of what her gasps are saying. He calls his married daughter from where she drinks ale, also his grandson of thirteen years busy celebrating the glory of a man's work. This farmer excuses himself from the Melliah but begs his neighbours to do justice to the spread. How clear we see the three of them, figures so tiny they could stand together on a nail's head. They enter the farmhouse, where all is quiet as Sunday: rugs spread on the floor, a fire banked up with turf, kettle singing from the slowrie, a fly measuring the quietness wall to wall, whips hung on pegs and boots hung on pegs, hats belonging to the working folk hung round the kitchen wall. In the quiet they share the news, the woman having only one question she needs to hear answered (just as the island has one mountain). Was young Hall arrested with him? she asks.

Are you there? Do you still hold the island in your hand, this model of order and the benefit of law? Evening stands around the house clear and fresh. Herring fishing ends for the season with the herrings salted down. Rooks caw and flap among elm trees at the edge of town. We see inside the Doolish Courthouse. A half-wheel section at the top of each window being propped open on a brass catch to let out the hot pleasure of spectators. Now the sun sets. Flames are brought for the candles while the High Bailiff announces a verdict. The spectators dare not breathe lest it be known what evil lurks in their hearts which they might not wish to let show. But one voice does speak out. My father, from the dock, replies in his quiet and casual way: Narra noain dhyt!

Do you hear that as you read my words? Do you know the grief we know? Does life mean what you thought?

Out into the night we take those words my father spoke, down along a shadowed lamplit lane beside the court house and into the black tomorrow: Your fate come on you!

On the Governor in Government House too, my mother adds, also a curse on the Atholls and the Stanleys of Derby.

You hold in your hand the harvest of order. If there is any pain in your knees from kneeling on the rocky coast of Britain, please feel free to set the island back among its waves, you need not bother with it any more, you may leave it to the mercy of contending enemies.

My brother escaped to sing "Finnegan's Wake" another day. But we never saw my father again.

I knew nothing of letting go. I was too young to imagine anything beyond the dead littleness of life: my routine as an apprentice, the craft I set out to learn, even my mother's promise that I would be a poet one day, considering my gift with words. Neat and tidy and all of a piece. How could I be expected to imagine what I found here: an endless land with a maze of jungle ridges fanning in every bewildered direction as various and grim as a choppy sea, where each landmark is set among a thousand thousands like it, or the inland plains under vast skies parading clouds that can be seen raining a hundred miles away, a continent of yellow-grey grass littered with pebbles which, seen closer, are bigger than barrels, bigger than carts, bigger than houses, until when you come right up to them they are too big and round to climb, but a dozen men may sit in their shade all day, gazing out at a galaxy of those other boulders you will never visit. All this was indeed a strange world. Back home I thought it a long way to walk the half mile downhill to Douglas and the half mile uphill for tea.

Printery—Established 1619. That was the sign outside our shop. I don't believe the machines had changed either. You could never call the island rich. Yet the printery produced work second to none, as we told our customers.

Thinking back, I begin to wonder whether a deeper promise already called me. Don't you see? Is there ever such an odd thing as chance? When I set up my forgery was I answering the promise though I had no idea I was hearing it? Was ignorance the one quality required by fate—the mere thought of my mother's grief would have bled me of courage—ignorance, and talent too perhaps? Talent because this is what led me to the wilderness. I was so steady that I was the only one let supervise himself. Every fact fits, right through to my chancing upon boxes of old blocks and packets of vellum in our storeroom. I was in full flight and headed for my downfall, my capture, my hurt . . . and my escape. The fact that I had courage put the issue beyond doubt and forced me to my destiny. The best laugh is that if I had been wild like Hall—neglecting to study, breaking my contract, worrying our mother out of her life—I might be there still to comfort her.

One skill I shall need to learn all over again, and you shall teach me, is to laugh. I do remember laughing and laughing a lot. More of this later. There are yet more confessions if I am to be honest with you.

We must go back to the fire.

Scrambling up the hill away from the smoulder and ruin, I knew I had been corrupted, the turmoil in my heart nothing more than mawky. Glimpsing the house as an idea I had had as a child took me back to childhood. I wept for my father. We were never to sing, for him, that he had a sort of tipplin' way, with the love of liquor he was born; and to help him on with the work each day, he'd a drop of the craythur ev'ry morn.

> Whack the folthe dah, dance to your partner
> Welt the flure yer trotters shake,
> Wasn't it the truth I told you,
> Lots of fun at Finnegan's wake.

I was not such a fool as to return to the fire and risk being caught, but I was curious to know if anyone survived and what they would do next; like being a child who learns by watching adults. Would they take the pinnace and chance the current, or would they wait for "Fraternity" to show up from wherever she had been, bringing whatever she was expected to bring? Did the Master survive and would he lie mending while he ordered the fence fixed, a palisade built and a new house begun? I hung around at the edge of the forest. I listened out for the signal of hammers and saws. I wanted to hear them.

What I did hear, one night, was a man crashing among the vines and bracken. I sprang up from where I lay. I crouched in the dark to listen until listening hurt. This was no kangaroo nor any native Indian. Dead boughs split and snapped under his boots, green sprigs thwacked at his clothes. He came right upon me, snuffling, letting out desperate grunts. He passed so close I could have tripped him. On he blustered. Keep going that way, I thought, and you will soon come up against a clump of trees grown so close together you will try in vain to force your way among them, tough stunted trees with papery bark flaking off them. He crashed ahead. He called out each time he stumbled but I could not pick any word I knew. Not one. I, who had been so vain because my mother boasted of my way with words! Well, those trees stopped him all right. I waited to hear what he would do next. I thought about my weakness and the cant of it. Was I still green? A million trilling insects left off their chorus too. We listened together. All quiet. He must have fallen. He must be crumpled there, beaten by the jungle, staying put until daylight. Exactly as I once did.

You will say I was mad to tarry, that no matter how swift I moved in the morning I must face the danger of being caught. True. But when dawn came I had not yet finished turning my thoughts to the dark. In the glimmer of morning the bush woke without charm. The overcast sky faded from the colour of soot to the colour of ash. I squatted in very much the place where I broke and slept that first night of my escape, hemmed in by dense tangles of dead and sprouting plants which, to my eye, matted like a tapestry without form, blocking the whole world, hanging from the sky right to the ground underfoot, so deep as to have no depth, so close as to be never reached. In effect a screen. Even though I made no move I knew I could walk into it when I chose and find the screen renewed yet still complete. This one skill I had learned—I could gain ground through that maze with scarce a rustle to give me away.

There was no mistake, the small furry animals sat tight and put off their usual business: an intruder lay there, less than fifty yards on.

Birds began their tit for tat while the light grew strong. The ocean still made itself heard, methodical and sullen along the beach. I stared near-sighted at where I knew he would be, alert for the first suspicion of movement.

So, I thought, I shall not escape, after all!

Looking back on it, I see that a deep need held me prisoner. Freedom is not the greatest force. The call came; more urgent than escaping into my chaos. Did I know what this was? Perhaps I did. Then again perhaps not. Yet I found the courage to face it, to put salvation behind me. Once my mind began slithering down the slope I gave myself to the thrill of letting go. Could that sleeping man be the Master, half-dead with wounds? Or was he an escaped convict like me? Of all questions the most curious was this: Would the fellow wake to find himself in a circle of Men?

I looked for them. I applied to my ears for what they might tell me. The air, full of chirrups and scuttlings, was void of human sounds—only that expectant stillness of an alien body just come to its senses, before it begins to stampede about, hunting for a path where paths have never been.

Not yet too late, I could still creep clear and make my escape along the ridge to the open forest. Instead, I plucked a couple of berries from a shrub, bit them open, dug out the pips as I had been shown, and ate the fruit.

He stands without warning. Though I have waited I am not ready. He is closer than I thought. My scalp freezes. I am spellbound. When he turns to look he will catch me. However still I stand I will never again have the skill of Men to be invisible. He has his back to me. He wears a thick shirt and breeches. The Master. Yes, he has the Master's build and rubs the back of his head with one hand. Surely this is what the Master used to do? The other arm hangs limp at his side. There is a message in the set of those shoulders which I can not quite read.

Still having time to duck down, to worm my way along a gully I know and give him the slip, I do nothing. The spell has its claws in me, because how could the Master be on his feet again and why come crashing through the wilds at night? He does not appear to carry a gun. But if he is looking for someone it must be me—or else why don't he call out? And why else stand so still? He is still as a hunter. This shocks me to my senses. Inch by inch I back away.

Leaves betray me with their whispering shadows.

He turns. He sees me. We are face to face. I squint to be sure of him. The sinister pull of the world of Easter and fairgrounds, of ventriloquists and devils on stilts, drains my heart to emptiness. He holds up his arm to arrest my escape: an arm without a hand.

Do you understand that even then it was not too late, because I knew that place and its secrets? How could I be stopped but by a bullet? I knew now what held me so enthralled. This was a dead man.

I waited for him to wade my way among tangled vines. And he did. He thrust himself mindless into the thicket and broke a passage through. Step by step I got him in better focus, that handsome fellow. With his cruel arrogance he had entered his own chaos and been lost. He peered out from under a jumble of hair, eyes anxious and glad. He uttered cries in a language I no longer knew, supposing I ever had known it. Yet the Master's curse, the previous evening, was not lost on me.

He reached with his good arm to grab me by the throat. You will hardly believe this, but I let him do so, being helpless with astonishment and in a sweat of terror. Then instead he took hold of my shoulder, his fingers still thick with strength. He pulled me to him until my face was close to his and stared at me, absorbed, taking in each feature.

He is remembering, I told myself, our three whole days together. He remembers his arm against mine when they clapped the manacle on us, the bashings, my humiliation, the effort as he jerked me to my feet for more punishment, my nose running, my secret tears. He remembers his fever and the onset of weakness. He remembers forcing my hand under him to clear away his filth. He is looking back to seek some clue which he ought not to have missed at the time, some giveaway sign that this cully was capable of rebellion. He remembers my dead weight smothering him. He may even have hovered in spirit above the deck to witness his hand chopped off.

Then I saw that he recognized nothing. I made to loosen his grip. As I lifted my arm he shielded his face.

This was not a dead man driven by unforgotten angers, knowing he once suffocated under my loathsome body. This was not a ghost hungry for vengeance. This was a man heavy with blood and solid in the early light, crushing the plants as he trod them down. He clung to me and cringed. Until that instant I do not believe I had reached the true bottom of anger since, as a boy, I had to stifle my helpless rage against a judge passing sentence on my father.

I had seen Gabriel Dean dead, and now I saw him alive. His legs were functioning, his eyes saw, his mouth opened and shut. If I punched his face a bruise would begin to gather. How this could be was beyond me, but without doubt Gabriel Dean did stand there, all the more certain alive because so changed. I had thought my adventure unique; I never expected to find that during the same period even stranger things might have happened to him. His cringe sent bitterness thrilling through me. Was I to be stripped of all I believed? Was I to be left with nothing of the past though I had paid my life to renounce that world of order? Might I not be spared the bully as a bully? Beauty as beauty?

One thing I did know: you can not be a leader and live in chaos as well. I struck his arm from my shoulder.

Keep off, I barked.

Cackles of mocking laughter came from the tree above us; it was those birds with their uncanny call, egging each other on as they do. He lunged at me with a cry that might be mistaken for misery, but I threw him back. My flesh shuddered at the touch of the unknown. He stood arrested, mouth sagged open. Wrist stump hidden behind his back, as though that might be to blame for my ill will, he made pleading gestures.

When I turned to go, Gabriel Dean followed. If I paused he paused. When I went on again he kept me at a fixed distance. He became a clumsy replica of me; and I could guess how my guardians must have despised my own early efforts. The faster I walked, though too proud to hurry, the more he crashed in my tracks, gasping and desperate but without complaint.

In this way I brought him to a pool. Water lay still and dark under the trees while at the far side reflecting bright clouds. I bent down to drink. I showed him how. But he propped. This he would not copy. He stood back from the bank, eyes fixed, wonderment around his mouth widening across his cheeks.

He took my leadership away from me.

I looked where he was looking: mirrored clouds slid

over the glossy water to vanish in a net of shade, glittering for moments like golden thorns. Drips fell from my chin to shiver the surface where swift circles opened, rings of dark ribbons and bright ribbons—gone—again the same repeated swiftness—while out at the brink even the glowing silent clouds were touched by a gentle waver. Bewitched, Gabriel could not hear me. He could not be persuaded he ought to drink. Even though I grew furious at his stupidity and so far overcame my fear that I tried forcing him to obey me. Feeling tall, I thought of throwing him in. I tried. But, to my shame, was unable to shift him. He did not argue, he just resisted. And had lost none of his strength. His body took root like a tree.

You could smell more rain in the air, yet it did not fall. I was hungry, which was bearable; and peevish, which was not. I felt ashamed of my petty feelings. Chaos is too large and simple to leave room for such childishness. The clouds billowed solid and grew dark as they slid across the pool. Yet still I could not persuade him to follow me away from the dangers of the coast and into the forest, where we would not be caught. I admitted that I wished to leave him and be free, that I had not asked for his company, that I knew he was dead, that I shivered when he took hold of me. All this being true, my course lay clear. What was to stop me going alone?

Evening drew in. I left him happy with a lens of cloud cities and cloud mountains gliding across it. I left him.

For years now (this being the length of time I put on

my freedom) I had gone where my guardians went and eaten the food they brought. Isolated as a king, I had done nothing for myself but wait and watch. Now I put this knowledge to good use, picking my own fruit and digging for roots. I profited by that copper nail, which I found still tucked in my tangled hair, when poking grubs out of the tree bark where they burrow, those fat pale caterpillars. I ate them raw. A nasty thought stopped my blood and interrupted my eating: I had only dreamed I suffocated Gabriel—dreamed it while awake—much as my mother walked about her business when asleep. Perhaps the problem ran in our family. Whatever had happened that night aboard "Fraternity", the man's mind had gone before his body could call it back. But did I know this? Could I be sure? I ought to go back and see. So I went, flitting among trees and under vines, noiseless as my teachers who had worshipped me.

Gabriel Dean was a burden. I wanted nothing more to do with him. Nevertheless, I took a few juicy morsels . . . and thus I set about throwing away my freedom, that total freedom of mine, that joy which I can find no word for. I was going to let him rob me of me. But why? Why should he not look after himself?

He had not stirred, of course. A dusky purple cloud slanted across the pool. At first nothing I could do would win his attention. Not until a glittering sheet of darkness folded over the surface did Gabriel take the food. As soon as there were no clouds left to watch he was pleased to have me back. Drinking, he made a thin greedy sound, quite a feminine sound, which he kept up from time to time between gulps. He took his food: the root, the pink mushroom, the tiny yellow plum, the leaf, and the grub. He refused nothing.

Since I was anxious not to be stuck at the pool all the next day too, I set off straight away. Up the ridge I strode, satisfied by hearing him follow. Then the awful truth of this staggered me: satisfied! Just so. And wasn't I already on the lookout for landmarks known to me, picking my way through the bush as if following a path? What next? Chaos with a path through it is no longer chaos. In the end any such path must lead me back, whether I wanted this or no, to the ruined farm . . . to a fence, to a window with bars.

Gabriel stopped. He shook his shaggy head. And spewed the food I gave him.

By the time we lay down to sleep I had only one thought left in my head: escape! I believe you will understand. I believe you will see that I had to save my life. Yet I lay, still awake, divided and uncertain.

At dawn, red clouds filled the sky above the trees. They sailed in from the sea, a dumb procession puffed up with dignity. Gabriel remained on his back, eyes as wide as they would go and a beetle drinking at a tear stain. No sooner did I decide he was dead than he moved. He lifted the arm without a hand and placed it across his chest. He did not turn to look at me even though I brought some berries. When I put food in his mouth he chewed. But he wasn't going to miss a single cloud. I asked how he felt this morning. He stared past me. I saw them there in his eyes—plump pink cushions in miniature, clouds to suit an island so tiny you could take it in your hand.

As for his hand, the lost one, it filled me with fear—being more there than the one he still had. I reminded myself that quite ordinary folk may have a hand missing. There was the mill worker who lived near the old Douglas crossroads and lost his in a crusher. There was the doorman at the courthouse even, whose one hand qualified him for work. Each of those missing hands meant a simple loss to the shrivelled arm inside a sleeve tucked in a coat pocket. Gabriel Dean's lost hand had become a mighty thing, the lone survivor of a lost body, a perfect cruel hand still full of the grace gone from the rest of him.

The distance boomed with muffled drums. I experienced an overpowering desire to smother him again. This time I would really put an end to the creature. I felt so strong. But first I must place my ear on his chest to hear his heart, to be sure he wasn't a ghost, because trying to murder a ghost might lead to problems. I looked up and saw what he was seeing: scuds of cloud with edges bright as knives. Again it was the silence of their passage that gave these giants such strange power.

I did not dare touch him. My needs went begging. To hell with the idiot, let him rot.

But I could not help myself. Something in my childhood made me stay and look after him. I hated him all the more. He would not get up. How was I to bring water to him here at the edge of the forest? The question fretted me as I set out, busy gathering more food for two. You see how quick I took to my new spunkless servitude? But no—there were strong arguments against delicacy.

Would I leave him or look after him? I could not decide. Even when I returned to place his share beside him as an offering. I set off again.

I was alert for signs of Men and often stopped to peer among the trees expecting to find my guardians in a circle around me. Or expecting they might switch their loyalty to the cloud-struck Gabriel. And that afternoon I did come upon some half buried embers of a fire. Still warm. The watchers were near, I could feel through my skin that they watched. But, all eyes though I was, I caught no glimpse of anybody.

Another thing: I found myself constantly pausing to check on the sky. These pauses grew longer. I saw fascinating banks of cloud drift and collide. The mere air grew in my mind to fill me with a drama of merging vapours. Next thing I had hurried back to Gabriel, master of clouds, to warn him that these pretty games of his were about to rain on us and the rain would be a downpour. Of course I was hoping he had got up and gone, died or become lost. Yet my heart jumped with relief when I saw him there still.

I bent over him—this man who once insulted and

oppressed me, this victim of my murder—careful not to get in the way of his sky. Were the true clouds happening in there: being born in his imagination and thrown up as giant shadows on a distant wall? Might he, in other words, be commanding this rain? Afraid to interrupt, I placed more food in reach and stood back to watch what he did next.

The downpour, when it began, made him blink. Was he a conjuror? Did it rain harder the harder he thought of it? A monotonous patter settled among the leaves. He blinked and stared and thought. Rain came teeming down. His clothes were soaked. Trickles of water ran under him where he lay. This time I did not lose patience. He was not clever enough to realize that if he made the rain too dense the sky would go a general grey, sink to the level of treetops and blot out his clouds. Finish. He turned aside from it and crammed some food in his mouth. So he had known all along: he had known I came and what I brought. I smiled. We were friends, then.

We slushed off on our journey together to the grasslands. I now saw that I intended to make a full circuit of the territory known to Men. This was my ambition. Gabriel would be shown what I had been shown. The gifts given me would be offered to him. I helped clear his way, pointed out pitfalls, chose the least tiring alternatives in that trackless country. And once, when we overheard people talk and laugh in the distance, I hastened towards them, never suspecting this might be dangerous, eager to show them that I was not a freak, that here was a fellow of my kind. How weak! I would present them with a friend who had proved himself the better man though I defeated him; who, now he had returned from the dead, must be kept alive. But the talk and laughter fled at our approach. No silent Men, part-tree part-bird, stood and watched or flipped spears off the ground with their toes. No one threatened us or tried to influence the way we took.

Gabriel spewed again.

You must understand me, I was not unselfish. I taught him to sip rain from tiny runnels coursing down the tree trunks. I began taking pride in my care of him, in my skill at finding food—the food he still could not digest—in my skill at choosing our direction deep through that confusion.

Three cloud-rich days passed. On the fourth, the sky filled up with white tops too massive to move. They bellied and sagged, billowing and building gianter than anything on earth, until Gabriel grew exhausted with the effort and fell into an uneasy doze. As soon as he slept his white tops collapsed, mountains broke apart and dragged away, leaving pink scars from horizon to horizon of the evening. Before sunrise he began on filling the morning with fog. When he cleared it, he must have been remembering a sandy beach because the blue sky was all ribbed and scalloped. As before, his duties lasted the whole day and he only got up at twilight, when there was nothing left to do. We walked under a moon with a halo, myself as guide and him still in the musing way of an artist who looks back on his inspirations. By the sixth day I found I had been leading us, aided by the call of soft constant thunder, towards a waterfall. We had come to a place I never saw before. The creek rushed solid down to a midway basin and then spilled over to plunge into a pool hollowed from rock. Fern trees grouped round this deep clear pool. Flowers grew from cracks in the cliff.

Naked I slid down the rim into the cold water. While my body sang at the delicious knowledge of what it was to swim I wept again for lost memories. I stayed near the edge, splashing, dipping my head for the amazement of water washing among my hairs, the freedom of feeling it lay them flat.

Gabriel looked hard at me when I crawled out. He was seeing me as he had not seen me yet. Did he recognize me without my disguise of filth? Then perhaps I should be ready for him to rise up and take revenge for his lost hand and lost mind. This made me nervous. I invited him to drink, squatting to show him how. He watched. But stayed where he was, propping himself on his one whole arm as he sat shedding sleep.

I knew I would accept my fate.

You see how far I had come since kicking the officers who dragged me from the courtroom at Oxford? I was not going to run away. Indeed I went towards him, my wet feet slapping on stone. So I found my courage at last—but only with the aid of poor sight, as the affair turned out, because once close enough I could see that it was not me he stared at. He stared past me to where the churning water smoothed to its edge as a clear surface holding the empty sky. That mirror was what he watched. The blank of his slow face opened out to terror. There was no sign of a cloud. The blue showed bluer the more I looked into it. Deep air stood steady. Gabriel refused to drink cloudless water.

My arms and legs gleamed. What did I have to be ashamed of? How else ought I to be? Wasn't it the wonderful comedy of the world that human beings are made of skin and hair, knuckles and nails?

Just as once he had been at my mercy thanks to the power of a fever, now, thanks to the power of the clouds in his brain, he was at my mercy again. If I led him on into the land of food which he could not stomach, offering him water he could not accept, I would kill him surely. He had no manacle to brandish, no power to make me do his will. How could I bring myself to murder him twice? What say we retraced our pitiful progress, turning our backs on this journey through the whole country of Men as I knew it—even supposing Gabriel consented to travel while the sun was up—I would still need to support him for at least two days before reaching the coast. Once there, I faced the risk of being captured, the Master surviving in some corner of his burnt anger, his agents returning by ship in time to charge me with the disaster.

Such ideas presented a set of pictures on stained glass. Myself depicted as a lesson for others.

The fact was that only Gabriel could save me from being a leader. The plan to return would fail if he dug his heels in and refused to follow. This was my chief hope when I set out without a word to him, my clean feet stepping delicate among roots and rotting mulch. I would test him. He was to be given a chance of redeeming my guilt by saving the man who had murdered him.

These are the things I need you to know.

I am just looking back over the last page and hoping I do not alarm you with my ideas.

Let me try to put your mind at ease. Through all my misadventures what troubles me most is that my folk have no idea what has happened to me. You may guess how a mother would feel. The blame must fall on the stubborn secrecy of my resolve to live up to my responsibilities. You see, I set and printed the Commentary upon the Thebaid of Statius entire in my own time at night and then signed it with the great man's mark. I could not confess to my mother or even to Hall what I had done. Anyway, I suppose it struck me as more of a prank than a crime. I felt damn clever too.

Did something warn me my skill might be out of hand and putting me beyond my depth? Not until I turned my back to the island. Fool youth though I was, my teeth did chatter when I set foot on the packet for Liverpool.

So how can I say I was innocent or expect you to believe me? Yet I do.

You may guess how proud our family was. Me, for a start, taking on the work of an English master to baffle a university dealer, hoping to return home with money for my mother now that my father's smuggling had brought him to the Earl of Derby's gallows. Madness. But I was full of vim and my childhood had been carefree. When anybody asked my name as I walked across country to Oxford I told them John (which it is not). When I was sitting in fatal comfort, hearing that little bell behind my back jiggle on its spring, the dealer looked past me to see who entered his shop and asked my name.

John Stanley, I replied pert.

The composer of "Oroonoko", I presume? he kept up the joke in a kindish manner. Oh yes, he was kind.

How should I have heard of any John Stanley except the first Earl of Derby, who took the title King of Man? Or any such thing as "Oroonoko"? Or any such person as Mrs Aphra Behn? Only when the Reverend Davies came aboard our transport at the Cape of Good Hope did I learn about Mrs Aphra Behn.

Throughout the trial they referred to me as the Supposed John Stanley. No torture would have wrung from me my father's name or mention of my village. Indeed, I told them that although I came from the Isle of Man I was said to have been Irish, an orphan born at Drogheda on the Boyne.

Even the Pope expressed satisfaction, the judge remarked, at the defeat of your people by William of Orange—what do you think of that, ay? But I suppose every kind of lesson is lost on you. Well this one won't be, let me assure the citizens of Oxford. We shall not be indifferent to the theft of any part of our national heritage. And Ireland being as much under English law as the Isle of Man, the citizens of Drogheda are bound and protected by the law to the same degree as these good people here.

So the joke was that I needed to prove my forgery was a forgery and not a theft. No one believed me. They mocked me for my presumption. I was even stood up in front of the court to answer the charge of throwing doubt on Caxton's fitness to produce one hundred editions. And now there was no point in calling attention to the concealed initials FJ, because why FJ if my initials were, as I told the court, JS? Yet anything was worth a try.

Well, said I, my mother christened me Felim John Stanley, so I've been told.

The best they could make of it was that this did amount to an answer of sorts; whereas there seemed no immediate answer to why old Caxton, whose mark was already so prominent as to risk seeming too forward, should slip in a secret FJ signature. I saved my neck by winning an appeal—this meant paying the only shilling I had as a bribe to be allowed to show my trade at a proper printery. And what a sharp place it was, with a score of the most modern presses.

I gave them proof that I was a forger and not a thief of treasures. My reward was to be sent in fetters to New South Wales.

I shall make you smile when I confess that there was a moment when the trial became so interesting that I began to enjoy myself! An expert was called in to give evidence on the latest craft of copying documents or works of art. He told us that in France is a camera obscura with this difference from ours—it can fix the picture inside by engraving a square plate of silver. Nor is this witchcraft. Even in England they have tried it already and made it work. He was a most honest kind of expert. He told us that with spectacle lenses such automatic engraving will soon make portraits and landscapes. I can't fancy how. But he said so. Imagine! Nature engraving herself!

I realize I ought to have called out: What will become of the law against forgery then? I ought to have said it. But I was too busy learning.

I once had the chance to look through some spectacles at the fair. I never saw anything more beautiful. Every tree had a hundred twigs. Birds could be seen flying high in the sky. A clown on stilts was pulling a face. They brought things so close that I could read the word FAIR right across the common.

At any rate, forgers are friends of the original. Why? Because the forgery is only worthwhile when the original is one of a kind. So a forger brings an artist respect. And yet judges do not have artists led away in chains.

Speaking of chains, I noticed on the manacle a locksmith's mark stamped into the iron: FJ. As if it had been made for me, forged for me, you might say. Even my imagination was given no room by fate.

As for guilt—and I must be frank about feeling guilt—I suffered horrors because that shilling had been borrowed, also a further elevenpence, from my brother's box of papers. I had not asked him; and now I might never be able to explain or pay him back. He will think badly of me. This reminds me of something worse, speaking of the box. Not only did I take his money but I also stole a look into his soul by reading a letter from some woman. Heart of my life, she wrote, and all mine, even your lovely goat legs, when shall we make the eight-shanked beast again? You are less my friend, she wrote, than the friend you keep hidden.

It astonished me how she knew about his hairiness. I guessed the friend he kept hidden might be myself. I could never ask him, that's obvious, but I still carry her words as a talisman. At work next morning I told the whole workshop that my brother would as soon make the eight-shanked beast as be seen in any church. I hadn't meant to let it out. But I did not expect what happened. I was caught by the ear and thrown into the street to enjoy some rain for half an hour. That should cool your blood, said the journeyman who bolted the door, and when I let you back you can keep your hands busy with cleaning the racks (these were racks where we stored the fonts) instead of taking your Saturday afternoon off.

She must have been an educated woman, that friend of Hall's, writing like she did in such a clear hand, though she was a hopeless speller.

I am sorry I took the cash. But I do not regret sticking my nose in his affairs. What else are older brothers for? And this woman's secret words are the only love letter I ever had the chance to look at. You see my plan? I sit here day in day out to work at the task of teaching myself to talk again. Soon I shall be ready for facing you in person, for the joy of hearing your voice and asking you to believe my answers to your questions. I tremble with excitement to think how great an idiot I shall seem. I imagine the things I shall find myself saying to you. Such things!

Gabriel, having excellent sight no doubt, could see what I could not. Yet all he did was watch clouds. And what use was that? For the most part he stumbled behind me, weak from hunger and thirst, shaking his head at the tidbits I found for him but alert if we came upon fragments of laughter still haunting the air, or the smell of roasted meat (probably the Master's beef!), as on the day we reached the coast again. I shrank smaller while he grew cheerful. He knew he was on the way home. Also he still knew what laughter meant when he heard it. I reckon that a person is never lost for good if he remembers laughter.

The moon set not long after the sun that night. Clouds stood up over a far-off sea as flat and still as glass from where we were. Gabriel gazed at the sight for an age. And when he threw himself down beside me on the tussocks I noticed the glass edge of his eyes. I wished he would eat but he would not. Neither of us slept, he in his grateful swoon, I weltering in fear at having risked my life to come back so near the Master's fences.

I pause here for a marvel: a void. I am at the brink of a chasm, pen in hand, because who knows what you think of this? Will I fly or fall? The only certain fact is that you are still reading. You might be bored, angry, disgusted . . .

At least, do you agree that it is best to face a crisis with laughter, leaping around as the mourners at Finnegan's wake leapt, welting the floor and drunk like the dead man himself would have been for sure. Well, you will excuse me the liquor I made free with this afternoon. As it happens I am not a man with a sort of tipplin' way. But what choice do I have? The writing comes slow in any case—with me sitting here and nothing else to do.

So, to press ahead. By dawn the chances of being killed seemed to outweigh any hope that I might deliver Gabriel to safety and get clear again. Either the Master's shot would get me, or a native spear. Yet not only did I still lead the way towards this fatality with a sort of pride at doing my duty but with a light-body feeling like expecting a birthday. Mad though this was for sure, it seemed to be catching. Gabriel's face broke with lopsided happiness while he watched me swilled clean and cavorting. I dug more caterpillars for him and picked more berries. He did not seem to mind that he brought them up as soon as he swallowed them. I looked on the bright side: this was all I could offer and at least he agreed to accept it. What's more, he drank again from the pool filled with clouds. If you ask me, his instinct told him he was well on the way home to bondage. No wonder he felt glad!

For a moment I suspected his happy mood had the same cause as my madness. Duty. Maybe he saw visions of the selfsame person, down there among charred rafters, aiming the same carbine. But the idea was fanciful. As a man in the full power of my intelligence, surviving adventures enough to kill many another, I put it behind me. We went forward.

Right there, in the middle of a place never tamed or tampered with, what should we come upon but a dead cow. The carcase had been butchered and singed, the hind quarters part buried in a trench of warm coals, perhaps still waiting to be dug up and eaten. The flesh was torn away from shoulders and flanks so the skeleton showed through and shreds of blackened hide dangled thick with ants. The cow's stricken face was turned up towards us, so you might think she still had life in her and she required an explanation of the horror—her horns alert, mouth open and the tongue gone. The head was propped up, as I then saw, by the shafts of some broken spears stuck in her neck.

A new era began.

Who was I to care? I pranced ahead in the grip of this ridiculous mood. You would have called me a child rather than a man of twenty or twenty-one (I cannot be sure which).

It occurs to me now that Gabriel's satisfaction might have been solely on my account, because at last he had me at the mercy of his will. So confident was he by this time that he stopped to gnaw the carcase, mad with gratitude, ravenous for half-cooked flesh of a taste he knew. As for me, I could never stomach such food again. I confess this to you so you will be ready for how strange I have become: a meal of moths is more to my liking.

Down through the clump of close-grown trees we wended, me slipping nimble among them, Gabriel crashing along, and into that tangle of undergrowth where I had found him, to the foreshore of flowered shrubs, to the embankment above the Master's logging camp, and to the Master's road.

The pinnace had gone.

This was as far as I would risk taking my charge. From here on Gabriel must make his own way. Hadn't I put myself in danger enough? (The proof is the four walls shutting me in now as I write.) I remember a cold shock of commonsense. What sort of rash fool presents himself a second time to be shot? Or to be chained, for that matter, or whipped as a deserter?

I had delivered him. He knew where he was. I wished him goodbye, patted his shoulder and turned inland again. But Gabriel caught that patting hand. He was already in the act of stepping down the embankment so I found myself wrenched and dragged, staggering on to the road. The animal in a trap knows everything in a flash. Fear of the trap is in our blood, known by the deepest instinct. I fought to shake him off. I lashed out at him, I twisted and cursed, I kicked and used my elbows. Most of these blows hit their mark. Still he would not let go. By now he had hold of my arm. I could not break his grip. The nerves were dead in him, most likely, because nothing hurt. He made no attempt to kick me as I kicked him. He did not even try forcing my arm the wrong way. He held tight and plodded ahead, fixed upon reaching the farm ruins.

While anxious to make as little noise as possible, I struggled like a wild thing. Once I tripped him and brought us both down among loose sharp stones. But he held me firm, lumbering to his feet with no resentment and taking up his task. If he had only conquered the fever and found strength sufficient as this aboard "Fraternity", he would have thrown me off easy and seen me hung. Waving that handless arm, although nobody appeared, he bundled me along.

All my energy left me.

The picture I must show you is of a clothed man bringing in a naked savage. This is a picture which we know from as far into childhood as we can recall, is it not? A British picture.

The beautiful chaos back there called. Birds with no name called. Scents never before smelt called. Greens not green and browns not brown, leaves hanging vertical from their twigs to cast no shade. The looseness of the place lodged in me as an ache. And where was my circle? I believed my guardians had seen enough by now to come and rescue me. I saw nobody. What use was their knowledge of eternity if they did not foresee this? I had proved my power to them. Who could take away from me those minutes when the snake peered in at my cry of fear in time to stop it coming? Who could deny that St Elmo's fire played about my head or that the lightning did not strike?

I knew then what I feared—not the Master and his carbine, nor being manacled to Gabriel's one complete arm—I feared being seen naked by a lady! Isn't that enough to make you sick laughing?

I offer it to you as the real test of whether a man is civilized.

Night again here in my confinement, with just enough of a fading dusk left to jot down another thought for you. This afternoon I wrote about the clothed man bringing home his captive and about my worry lest I was caught naked. I should make clear that the people I have been living among wear no clothes. Even their feathers and bunches of leaves are not placed to cover nakedness, being mainly decorations on the head, arms, chest and thighs. Also I must report that after only a few days, to my surprise, I no longer noticed this.

I was brought up a modest boy. Therefore I believe others would find the same thing and soon get used to it. I put it to you that when we give up the habit of clothes, you will scarce notice—provided the weather stays warm.

Mind you, if it became general, this would end the comedy of fashion. A terrible pity too. There is nothing at heart funny about the body, which is either beautiful or tragic, whereas clothes are always good for a laugh. Frilly bits and fur lining, the responsibility of matching one pink with another and risking eternal damnation if the length of a hem is not right. True, without clothes, people's lives must lack passion and scandal. Not to mention a severe shortage of jealousy and snobbery.

Yes, I take it back. Who cares if nakedness would soon pass unnoticed among them? Let them have their foibles. Let bottoms be all the more padded and waists pinched. I am starved of laughter. We cannot have too much laughter.

But for you and for me—good night.

Morning.

Lord, let me know mine end, and the number of my days: that I may be certified how long I have to live.

Isn't this the prayer everyone prays? Such folly—to hope that if once we were prepared, being allotted a fixed span, we would live more contented and die without anguish! The fellow who wrote the Psalms knew how to get under your skin.

As to Gabriel and me, wasn't it true that for both of us our return might well number our days and no mistake? Bearing in mind the lessons of religion, no doubt my own end ought to be sweetened by the satisfaction of bringing a runaway back to the fold. Wasn't it worth losing my freedom to take his away for ever?

Instead, my capricious heart, my despot, felt sad. Seeing the wreckage of the place did this to me.

So the Master dreamed about Virginia, did he: rich plantations, a neat church, labourers singing in the fields? In his dream I suppose he saw himself looking up along this wild coast to where an orderly town might be built, where ships might tie up to a stone quay and dandies doff their hats to ladies. Or perhaps he dreamed of Jamaica: black slaves flocking down a hillside of tobacco fields, the women's laughter on a fruity breeze, tools being stacked in the barn where hogsheads would be broached and the slaves allowed their songs and dances under supervision, just a few heads needing to be clubbed before the procession could set out from the church to the waterfront, a statue of Christ with actual hair, a general looming of hysteria, candles in branched candlesticks guttering and smoking inside little glass chimneys, and a fantastic voice from the crowd singing lewd wild things from a fog of incense, but fear of the lash holding them, at last, in check and the day passing off with no more than a couple of deaths, the crop safe picked. Or did he dream the town as a planned place right where his gutted house is now, with civic offices each side of a clock tower, taverns on corners and a chapel behind? Well, what he achieved was one erect wall in which a single pane of glass held good, the charcoal shell of half a dozen outbuildings and kitchens, two standing sheds, one with the roof half gone, the other intact, a stockyard where a dead white horse lay as close to the water trough as it could stretch, and an empty paddock closed in by a broken fence.

I do not mock him. My own dreams are too breakable.

While I pause a moment I hear, down at the cove, that loose raft of logs clocking as the tide comes in. There. And again.

Yet I have not finished telling you about my return to the farm and Gabriel bringing me. Once I had stopped struggling he let me go. So simple. He was not bringing me against my will. He wanted me to be glad. I suppose he wanted a friend. So tight had his grip been all this while that I still felt fingers around my arm—as if he held me now with his missing hand. The place was deserted. Even the bodies among the ruined buildings were gone. Someone survived to bury them. I walked wary. Then a teasing thought came to my head. What if Gabriel had been neither lost when I found him in the bush nor wasting time hunting me but had offered himself as bait, certain of my being out there and certain that when I heard his blunderings I would be too curious to pass up the temptation of seeing who it was?

Do you notice that, released and given this further chance, still I did not learn, still I did not seize my freedom and clear out?

All I could think was that the farm and sawmill being abandoned provided proof that he had not run away. He had been left. Why this filled me with such fury at the time is hard to say. My life was always rich in lessons, yet it struck me as brutal that whoever took the pinnace did not take him along too, this broken soul, dumb with surviving the deep fears his body must remember from being murdered.

Gabriel himself knew enough to spend some minutes scanning the sea, seeming to expect their return. I was ashamed at suspecting him of treachery. He needed me. So great is his heart, I said, that he can find it in him to love any person who fills the void, no matter how base. He showed me (me, first among enemies) a nest in the part-standing hut, his dirty heap of rags. Then he guided me to the shed, the sole structure left untouched by fire, waiting in attendance while I unbolted the door.

I peered into a darkness smelling of sheep oil and stale

smoke. By the stripes of daylight slashing across the room from gaps between the planks I soon came to see what was there: twenty pair of folded blankets—a hundred pair maybe—suits of clothes, boxes full of gift knives for natives, scores of tomahawks stacked on a shelf among looking-glasses for native ladies and a heap of scissors. On the floor stood the station flour stock in sacks besides casks of grog, biscuits and salt beef. I could also see that the place was built of the stoutest timbers to foil theft and withstand attack.

My amazement that the Indians did not plunder this store gave place to respect: they had not wished to steal, despite a good portion of their land being stolen, they just wanted back what had been theirs before. The gift trinkets were doomed to remain covered with dust. Or was it more like a question of ignorance, the Indians failing to imagine what all this stood for, flour being foreign, corn being foreign, even the idea of things stored in one place foreign, and bribery being foreign too.

On a small table I found account books. Also a tray of paper, several jars of ink, some nibs and a pen (the very pen I am now using).

Gabriel stood back while I poked around. We had all the time in the world. And yet I scarce lost a minute before giving in to the old corruption. Torn between longing to set a mark on paper—a single letter of our alphabet would do—and the need to cover my nakedness, I took a shirt from the pile. I slipped my head in its noose, arms stuck up in the air. During those few seconds when I was blind and helpless he ducked out. The door swung to. The bolt shot home. So much for Gabriel being simple! This was my punishment for treating him like a child. Fury softened to fear. Trapped: I had put myself right back where I started in Oxford. Just as the dealer tricked me into the wasted time of being polite, so Gabriel Dean did the same. Our manners are a weapon against us.

There was no use banging on the door. I stood still to think. Hollow.

A haunting odour mingled with the sheep oil and smoke, some delicate thing of suggestions. It took me back to memories of our linen drawer on the landing in the Kirk Braddon cottage on the Isle of Man. Could there be a bag of dried herbs here among the blankets? Yet no sooner had I named the memory as herbs among linen than my nose lost it. The faintest trace, like an echo, seemed to linger on, a mere suggestion in my wishful thinking.

Nothing could be done until the gaoler came back with food. I felt sure he would come back because, if he was deft enough to throw a bolt, he could be nowhere near as helpless as I had thought. And he must want me alive, or why use so much cunning to entice me back, why not kill me out there where my remains would never be found?

You will know me well enough by now to see how typical it was that I took refuge in sorting through the choices offered. One was a plan to trick him by showing myself as his creature, being dressed in clothes and having a weapon already hidden among them. Another was to use a tomahawk and begin hacking away a section of wall. No, I must think of something quieter, something giving Gabriel less time to be ready to murder me the instant I showed my head. The best way out, I decided, was through the door. Meanwhile, I had to keep him calm by doing nothing. There was no hurry. It would be too much bad luck for the pinnace to arrive back right then. In any case, the sensible idea was to break out after dark. While puzzling over these plans I occupied myself by getting dressed. How strange it felt. The stuff touched me where I was tender. I tried sitting on the stool and remembered this too. What a great satisfaction it was to rest my elbows on the table and find it just the convenient height. I fitted a nib to the pen, dipped it in the inkwell and made a mark on a sheet of paper: I.

The thing looked graceful, a tiny vein traced down the middle where the nib spread at the top of the stroke. My eyes swam with longing. I think I was never so homesick as at that moment.

I heard Gabriel come stumbling around. I called to him with more pleading in my voice than I wanted him to hear. He did not answer.

I can tell you the exact moment when I knew you were there. Of course I can.

I confess it took me a long time to solve the mystery of that trace of fragrance which came and went several times. Once it happened when a bird sang, once when a shadow passed, interrupting my slit of light. But you must excuse me—how could I guess there might be a lady out there still in that wasted havoc? I failed to read the signs.

The day after I broached the grog and biscuits I heard a voice. Quite a long way off. At first I took it for an effect of the sea. You must have noticed hearing a lonely cry when at sea, or the chatter of crowds, only to find no one there. Then I knew, from the matter-of-fact tone. This voice was a voice.

To go by the rules the Master laid down before we set sail from Circular Wharf, any woman joining our enterprise must do so within the strict rules of decency—as a wife wedded by Christian wedding to the man she came with. Only one such woman sailed aboard "Fraternity".

So I knew.

The fact is that I could not discover any surprise at you being here. Once I realized this I knew I was expecting you. This expectation had tugged at me in secret to draw me back under false colours as Gabriel Dean's guide and protector. He had been more in my power than he knew. So! What do you make of that?

The door closed. The bolt shot home. I was captured again. But this time I was not your husband's prisoner. That fragrance kept me from despair. Again and again.

Until my being shut away began to take on new meaning. My mind filled with other plans and guesses, nothing to do with escape.

No sooner did I pick up the pen than I felt joy go wild in me. I had been given a purpose. Selecting a clean sheet of paper, I commenced with a sentence I mulled over for hours to get right. I must face the fact that you will have forgotten who I am. And look how many pages I have filled since then in order to put the full stop which I now make on this one.

Heart of my life. If only I can think clear I shall know what to say. I am breaking rules. These letters do not attempt to put our lives in order. They are part of the muddle. And part of the muddle of all letters this moment crossing paths in that terrible scramble forever going on throughout the globe. They are meant to throw you into utter confusion.

I have set down my faults and my claims as true as I am able. How delicious the hope that you will find in my confusion a new country to claim as your own and possess.

Will you forgive me my goat legs, my scaly hands, my beard grown thick, and my childish dumps? I promise to be happy.

My dearest,

One favour I beg: do not be too proud. My pain brings me some slight pleasure. But pride, in you, can only bring you loneliness and power.

We cry out when hurt. This is natural. Forgive me, then. Even heroes whose deeds set them far above us must be the same as other men: they must suffer or we would not recognize them as heroes. This is my excuse. You nor I can afford to seem polite. Only a barbarian dies smiling.

There, you see how I have conned my book of "Heroes in History and Fable"!

The one fact I can not escape is that you never come. This cold tap fills my veins. The terrible harmless cold goes pumping through my whole map of loneliness.

How disgusting that I go on living. Why won't I die? All I have, cooped up in silence in this mockery of gaol, is my own stench. Was it for this that I stepped over the gunwale of the boat, let myself be lifted on a wave of courage, and kept going up the sand, though I knew any escape into so strange a place would be an act of treachery?

Under my belly, while I strove to keep it soft enough for my crime to succeed, I felt Gabriel Dean's nose press against me, his brow, his chin. His mouth was moving.

You can not imagine the anguish you put me through. Nor how I fear that you may not be trying to hurt me, that you may be doing it because you feel nothing at all.

Our Lord, so the Psalm tells us, shall go up on high and He shall take captivity captive. I know how this feels. My present captivity has no power to confine me. Here in this dark store, among the paltry sort of gifts we offer in return for the luxury of being destroyers, I have reached the freedom to say what is in my heart.

In the courthouse at Douglas I sat on a wooden bench. My fingers played with a fold in my mother's skirt. Up there in front stood a man with shoulders bundled into a jacket too small for him. The suit was made of some rough woollen stuff. His hair had been wetted and brushed to one side above a face which was a clumsy wooden copy of my father's face. When asked to speak, the marvellous wooden mouth opened and there was even a ventriloquist voice that came out parroting my father. I looked round for him so we could smile together and I could let him know I thought this pretend person looked idiotic.

Speakers droned on. Much later the ushers brought light for the candles. The man in the woollen suit was led away. My heart stopped in a grip of ice when on a sudden he came to life and in my father's strong clear voice called out: Narra noain dhyt! and that toy face broke into my father's wonderful fierce smile.

My mother, who had been soft and absentminded, not too interested in what was being said, jumped up. Tremendous tall and proud she was as she marched me out through the crowd without a word about why they stared at us. Only when we reached the lane with its dingy lamps sputtering did she start sobbing sobs that stood my hair up under my cap.

Let me tell you I was surprised when I set eyes on Sydney. We were brought in right alongside the wharf. There was none of that clambering down rope ladders to board a lighter, an awkward matter after being shut away in the dark. They marched us along a plank in comfort. You will scarce believe I felt like singing.

So this was New South Wales, the exile we feared.

Across the harbour lay a peaceful ridge where a couple of windmills turned slow, also a church and a scatter of houses, each house with its own field. I could not make out more detail than this, but it all appeared pretty well established to me. Light grey drizzle gave the place a dismal aspect. The water was heavy as lead. Our side of the harbour being built as a stone quay, on which we stood, a fully paved roadway led up to the town. I had expected a tropical stone quarry where chained skeletons swung sledgehammers—anything but hansom cabs lined up outside solid buildings, gentlemen on horseback, ladies with umbrellas, and sailors unloading crates of cargo. At one doorway stood a queue of respectable people getting wet. A dog curled for shelter under a barrow. Merchants wore top hats, if you please, and frock coats. The port presented a forest of masts and spars asway on the tide while rigging slapped and hulls nudged the timbers with much bumping and squealing. The whole place was alive and going somewhere. Even the horses trotted with purpose.

Curious, though, the buildings already needing repair. You could not miss noticing. And we are uneasy with the decay of the new. The whole port—not yet fifty years old—had a worn-out look. That is how I saw it. But it smelled good. It smelled of horse dung and chandlery. Not like Douglas or Portsmouth (where we sailed from), which smelled of dead fish.

How does my sketch strike your memory?

Voices were shouting, such voices I had never heard—men become bulls. This was my first taste of what the next week in barracks confirmed. A fellow here may be respectable without hiding the beast in him. Or a woman too, for that matter. Everyone had someone to bellow at, warlike bellows, most of them, bullying and cheerful. Even the redcoats had showed up different the moment they stepped ashore. There was no mercy to be expected of them, as we knew already, but here they had no need to bother hiding it behind a mask.

So this country, I said to the next man, is a place to be reckoned with?

He spat in my face.

It was one of those fresh damp mornings. The drizzle had just stopped and some young ladies were braving the puddles to come and look us over and murmur sentiments of a Christian kind, nothing of the warrior or the beast to be seen in such modest girls. One of them took up my case and rounded on the fellow, telling him he deserved no better than a harsh task. Being spat upon, as I could have told her, was the least of it. He did not seem to hear. We just stood there, chained hand, foot and neck. She was a most uncommon young person. You could see she would soon make up her mind to something. She glanced about like a nervous hen, pretty as you like, then darted forward. Her eyes were fixed not on mine but somewhere in the region of my shirt button as she reached out with her handkerchief and poked at the mess on my face. It must have been torture for her, she went so red. She wiped it off and flung the handkerchief away. I watched the white thing flutter down into the harbour and settle on the water where a bitten apple core bobbed beside a drowned cat among curds of scum. Next thing she burst into tears and buried her face in her sleeve for lack of a second handkerchief. I never saw so tender a nape. I decided she was eighteen—like me—but I dare say she was less. How hot my face was. She hastened off with an older lady in a bonnet, leaving her handkerchief afloat on some bright little ripples slapping against the quay. When they marched us away I thought of my wet feet squelching on the exact same stones where her dry ones had trod.

By God's mercy the fellow who spat was drafted to a different gang or she would have had me murdered for her tenderness.

For as long as you keep away you can not complain if her voice is the voice I hear as yours, your hand the hand I feel wiping my cheek, your eyes the eyes I see cast down so modest. Does this make you fierce?

My love,

Love is what I hope to learn from you. Isn't it true that your body, like mine, rebels against being lonely? To have left you here alone, your husband must be dead or insensible. I mean insensible to your rebellion too. Dare I say so? My sufferings are enough to justify me.

This stuffy hole is dark with the beat of my heart and the thudding sea. Wherever you hide, out there among the ruins, your heart keeps time with mine. Feel it now. You can not escape me. If I am a prisoner, so are you. And I thank heaven for my new imprisonment anyway. Do we not all wish to return to our past for the chance to live it again with the wisdom of later experience; even to suffer the most painful bondage and find it blessed?

I think about your body and the mystery of it.

If you ask me my intentions, I intend having no limits.

My brother is a good man (if he has stayed the way he was) and I hope to prove as good. But I must confess to you that the act of love is the thing, and it is one thing I don't know that I know the first thing about.

My body is still a stranger to me. I knew my body when I was a boy but not any longer. Its shape and length of bone, hanks of hair and ugly health are none of them the way I thought manhood would come to me. Only my smell is homely. We do what we can to be as we wish, but Nature goes its own way. Did you lose the girl you were? We must talk. As for me, I had a fine idea of just what I wanted. Foolish hopes. The mischance is that we grow to hate the half-and-half mongrel so many of us find we become . . . all the more when we notice ghost reminders of our grandparents too.

Forgive my goatishness before you come to look at me. If you will, then I shall forgive your beauty.

What next?

I am caught. I must confess my needs. To declare myself. I come to those lovely simple names we have for making love and for the tools of it. Each like the blemished note of a bell. Such a coward I am, I dare not write them for fear they might ring too cold and vigorous. Shall we be free to say them when we are together?

If I make myself a fool here it is from respect for you. Those solid simple words must wait until we are face to face. All I shall promise is the violence of my body, which makes me gentle. I believe I might explode at your first touch. So you see how little of you I need use up! One touch. Only promise me we shall make the eight-shanked beast: and you shall find I can please you. The flesh, being fixed in its designs, sets the mind free to be tender. Please have no fear that I would hurt you. I beg you to judge my passion by my courtesy.

Dare I call you my love yet again?

You are still reading.

If I understand the poets, perfect love is an island. But not like the islands we know when we are children, each with its safe sea around it. Each with its sad coop of freaks whose babies are doomed to repeat the same freakiness. On this island we have come to, how else should the lions be but feathered red and green like parrots? The horses here damn well ought to grow horns and fight in battle like the men on their backs. In this place there might as well be all tongues spoken or none. Dwarfs and giants will of course be met with and sacrifices fed, as they are in fairytales. The place is open to those clean dangers gone from our modern world since pleasures began to be made in factories. What else should forty-two kings do but bow down to the one who loves?

We need never again be alone, you and I, from the moment when you call upon me.

You might not guess from these careful words but I am become lunatic. Shut away in here I speak filthy things. I sing for you. I lie on the floor, too weak to stand. I am driven to get up and to scrawl yet another pitiful secret letter. I pardon myself by saying that the longer you put up with me the better my opinion of myself and the greater the opportunity I am giving you to prove your greatness of heart.

Take me. I do not question the world's judgement that I am least and ugliest among men, a forger and a convict.

This, I put to you, is the very reason you should accept me.

Can you imagine how caring the forger must be, how exact with his craft, how much in love with what he does? First he must grasp what he is to achieve and then keep this general understanding in mind while he goes over the parts in finest detail. He must look into each detail to see details within a detail. He has to love the whole piece in the very act of loving these details within details, otherwise he will never make a forger. And where he finds a fault in the original he has to feel joy; and the same joy at making the same fault. The artist may be dissatisfied and unsure. The forger is his opposite. The forger knows just what to do and has perfect confidence in the work the artist does. The forger is a happy man. He is generous and easy pleased. He is not jealous of the original, he loves the original. He is not profane against God, because he does not presume to put forward rival creations. Last, he is a stickler: if his labour is to pass for the real thing he can not leave off halfway, as the artist might; he can not allow himself to falter.

This is the kind of man who writes to you, using words to take captivity captive.

As to my eyesight, you may know that the sufferer of my complaint has compensations, his near sight being exceeding sharp. By nature he can see such fine points as others may detect only with a magnifying glass. His hearing is acuter, his sense of smell more delicate. Agreed, the universe beyond reach of his hand loses its detail and fine lines: yet he recognizes a garden as a garden, a church as a church and a mountain a mountain. A tree may be a block of foliage and never a thousand leaves, but it is still a tree. The near-sighted person moves in a bubble of complications through his simplified world, more aware of being private than others and less brash in what he claims to know. Before he leaps he does his best to look. You may think him a sorry creature, yet he knows himself. This he does know. This is within his range of clearness. Dear love, believe me.

I have returned from peering out through the crack. I heard a flock of birds fly away chattering, headed for the forest. The thought of it makes me anxious. I want my own freedom, please. The land calls. But I shall not expect you to feel the land as I feel it. There is plenty of time. And I am used to being questioned. You may ask what you like.

If you are hoping for a slave, let me say that I have served my apprenticeship. If a master, I have studied with qualified tyrants. Allow me to go further. Suppose you want both: a slave one moment and a master the next; then who better for your purpose than a forger?

Can I believe what my heart tells me, that you watched your husband die? Was this because you wished him to die? Was his death not enough to touch your pity? Was it your plan to have the native Indians swarm down with flaming torches and leave his dream gutted because he dared make a dream beyond the dream of keeping you? Did your blood rejoice when you heard the spears hiss, when you saw him lured out from cover to kick a powder keg in among the cinders as his desperate bid to frighten them off before they finished him? Did you feel the first spear dig into him? Was it joy you felt? I can understand it. Another. Another. Had you known you were trapped in the prison of his needs? Had you confined yourself to narrow hopes so the soul might survive by scarce breathing, by drifting with the tide, by not even wasting the energy needed to call for help? I understand.

At first when I knew it was you I saw rush along the road from the jetty I thought you were sleepwalking. But I once knew a sleepwalker and how she walked. She never hurried, that one, nor did her breath come so fast. You may not have guessed I was there when you passed me in the dark. Well, I am used to the night. I am used to its faintest noises. The flapping of a skirt astounded me. Meanwhile, your husband lay clutching the knife he got off me. I would not put it past him to notice if it had once been his own and might have been filched. Was he base enough for this? Was he dying? Were you flying there to help? You know best. I only ask because I want to understand. And I believe you will agree that love admits no moral; just a body which takes—and gives nothing in return.

You can not shock me. My love will swallow all. As yours will too if it is to be love. I welcome whatever horrors I must suffer for your sake. If you agree to accept my beaten face and my back, raw wrists, the hump of hate in me and the jealousy. I would have them doubled to test your taste for me. I would have my sores break out again and suppurate, I would crawl in fear and commit the basest acts of cowardice just for the joy of entertaining you with nonsense.

Say nothing but vile things. Beauty added to your beauty would pile too much grief on me, making me falter under such happiness enough to remember who I am.

I shall prove I know you better than you believe I can. There is a precious secret between us which at all costs I swear to keep from the world. A few steps closer to the blaze, staring at what the flames themselves were showing you, I reckon you stopped. Is this right? I stopped also, in terror that you had seen me. I did not look round, let me be honest, but I heard the harsh sound of your lungs and heard it falter. At that same instant I heard something else too: the tumbler clicked against the sear when you cocked your pistol. You let out a hiss of air, closer to fury than to fear. I heard powder being tapped into a pan, no mistake about it. None. And then the stuff of your skirt slapping against your legs as you hurried on, with all in readiness.

Was your bullet to set him free, or to set you free? I

ask it of my heart as a conundrum with back-ways of delicious doubt.

How did you know to take a weapon with you if you had left your husband's bed before the attack began? On the other hand, if the attack had begun, how strange that you left at all. And stranger still that you did not rouse him with warnings.

This is my treasure.

I have confessed to you how I murdered Gabriel Dean, how I found him alive again and fell victim to his trap or to his need (it scarce matters which), never doubting myself. Why? Because the body willed it. I was drawn by the magnet of your nearness.

So now, when I declare myself your lover, do you begin to realize what I mean? As I write, the truth comes in a flash: you—the only white woman for a hundred miles—killed your husband for my sake.

Dearest. I am thinking I should rip the whole thing up. Tell me I have not lost you. What I wrote about your husband was because he did not deserve you. Also because the spark of fire I saw passing me in the night could have been his fire in the mirror of your eye.

You are passing me still, forever passing. And taller than I thought. You were outside my wall an hour ago. Your perfume haunts the place. Someone else came after you and tried the bolt. How many people are out there? So easy it is for fancies to become fears.

But should you have taken my part? I was honour bound, as the second bridegroom, to do the deed myself.

Again and again I tried to see your face. You were on the wharf at Sydney and you turned away, as a flurry of that amber dress, settling yourself in a landau while I caught only a whiff of your light. Once aboard ship, when sailing out through the Heads and the hatch was not yet closed, I glimpsed you gazing astern at the wake. Thinking of England, I suppose. Or grieving for some lost lover? You had a flower in your hand. Do you remember? These are fragments I treasure. Also your fantastical moans through the swaying pitching nights and that same voice, one day, speaking sharp to a sailor. Then came my last glimpse, when you were ill and being helped down the rope ladder. That is when you gave me a gift! You filled the Master's arms. He had to give you his complete concentration while keeping his balance. The boat rocked and yet he did deliver you safe to bondage. You gave me the gift of those minutes I needed in which to claim my freedom.

You see how much we have between us? This is my hoard of treasures. And of course there was the outline of your back, seen against the fire: yes, the truth is that I did look, once I had begun running again. I glanced over my shoulder and saw your back bent over, engrossed, while lightning flashed around you. Were you unscrewing the cap and shaking out more silver powder? What did you think about? The task of priming that pistol? Or the prospect of what you had to do? So it is your back, above all, which I remember.

I am in a rage at knowing this. As I bring the scene to life again I want to shock you into turning round and seeing me.

He did not love you. He did not. I will never believe he did. So—have you made love to yourself? Or will it be the first time when you come to me? I wish I could be forty, with the gift of experience to give you as well as the gift of my youth.

My angel of the sharp tongue,

I dare say you will be curious to hear what I did out there during that tribal journey, having so much time on my hands. The answer is nothing. Well, I believe I was born with a gift for indolence, thanks to which I could go blank enough to be open to knowledge. The knack was admitting that there can be no such thing as the discovery of a land. Does this surprise you? Granted, we hear tales pitched at having us think there is nothing in the world so interesting, from big discoveries by Marco Polo and James Cook and company, down to little places called Somebody's Folly. But what do discoverers do? They put names to landmarks unknown to them and not named by anybody they ever heard of. But do we imagine the Cape of Good Hope came into being just to be called that name? We might as well talk about the discoverers of ignorance.

All that happens is that words and numbers are written down. The chart is a big blank except for a squiggle of coast here and a river mouth there: a scatter of names on a clean expanse of ignorance.

You will object that Botany Bay, for example, was discovered by Cook because no other Englishman landed there before him in time to call it Dog Inlet. True enough. But what did he do when he chose the name? The place knew nothing of Botany Bay. He put a dabbler's limitation on it; and admitted he had such a poor huddle of categories in his mind that this was the best he could do for the infinite strange place he chanced upon. Bay, cove, inlet, sound, gulf, kyle, harbour—what else is there? This little list will do. You see my point.

So while the place crowded his senses with a thousand impressions, a riot of bird song and busy animals, wind among forests of chance leaves (let alone the massed ghosts of the dead and the unborn crowding upon his spirit), he ties it to the noble ideal of greed. How can this place be used? It is a bay. He does not hesitate. He invents what he sees. Nothing was here before he came. He knows this because the chart is blank. He takes an accurate bearing and writes numbers among the words. He takes up his pen (as I also hold mine) and prints BOTANY BAY—so many degrees so many minutes south, by so many degrees so many minutes east—where before this there was only untouched ignorance.

For my part, I hope to show you something less simple about the country we are in, something outside the categories you know. The day will come when we shall have space to discuss this. My wedding gift to you will be to open your eyes to the beauty of things without meaning or use.

When it comes to the issue of two worlds I can not sit by. I must take part on the savage side of the question.

As for James Cook being rowed ashore by sailors with hats and striped vests. You can see them in your mind's eye with their trews rolled up. Their bare feet splash in the shallows while those still aboard are shipping oars. You can look out at them from the shore and watch them reflected in the broad mirror of wet sand when a wave pulls back. The ship is at anchor in a deep channel. You can watch the great man leap out—success makes him young and springy—wading ashore to print the sand with the first boot mark ever made here. Well, aren't a hundred other eyes also watching? Don't the ocean wash away the imprint?

Nevertheless the first boot, being the first boot, you argue, must have been important.

Did it not take aeons for this place to be created, I reply, is it not old as the stars? So, what about a boot mark in the sand now?

We shall have wonderful arguments.

Let me give away all my secrets! I plan to stand by and wait until this land, which is so near you and so unseen, enters your heart too. I shall be there to whisper then that it needs no names. Your husband has had you in bondage to his cause of creating a counterfeit England by cutting down strange trees and digging out plants with no name. He has had you in bondage to the comfort of being able to call this thing a cabbage, this thing a peapod; of fencing animals you can call a cow, a horse, and keeping them fenced in case they recognize freedom with less trouble than civilized man.

This I can offer you.

I have already lived a life of knowing about marked limits and being kept in or kept out—of family and foreigner, owner and thief, tax agent and smuggler, artist and forger. But answer one question: Who makes the rule that certain things may be copied and certain things may not?

Each moment of life out there inland of that ridge is new. On my journey, gathering time, this was what I came to know. You can predict nothing. So much happens that your body tingles. The newness invades you, not just by the nine openings but by hundreds of nerves, thousands of hairs and pores. The person who is determined not to limit the risk is set free by risk. The body is part of the risk. So I can say that in my life up there I discovered nothing. And, at the promise of setting you free too, my heart sings. This will be my gift.

I wait for you.

Some days I have stopped writing because I could not go on without a drink. All I had was grog. And, my darling one, I have sworn to woo you sober. Being thirsty for so long and grown giddy from lack of water, I have promised to believe in God now the rain is beginning again, and for the moment I do believe. Sticking a knife through the roof, I have made a nice little trickle here and I am using a hat for a basin.

The light is awful poor. I work with my nose on the page.

You do not come.

I think of that sunk barque and those who might have gone down with her.

You must have noticed that I whittled a slot in the west wall, the wall without shelving. I can see out. I see, for a start, the dead horse still there.

I want to be seen myself. I want to be known. I want to feel what it is to offer my body. I want your cool fingers to touch my arm. The memory of that young woman's handkerchief on my face sends fires racing through me. So I know what I am talking about.

If only Gabriel would pass by, I might make him understand how to undo the bolt. Or at least he could deliver these letters.

And with them my love.

Heart of my heart,

I heard you at the door last night! I blessed myself for not giving up. I might have broken free on any day, armed as I am with more weapons than a man can carry.

In matters of love I admit I am an apprentice. But so was I an apprentice forger—and I foiled the experts. What a laugh. And I am happy now. You did not stay. But you came. You listened and then crept away on tiptoe. I called. You ran. You know this is the truth. The thing is that, when you ran, you ran with my message in your ears. You had to carry it with you. You could not escape without it. It must have filled your head, so big it was. I have nothing to add. That was my whole message: I love you.

My plan is to stay awake all night, waiting until you come again.

My dear one,

There is no use lying or pretending. My visitor was not any other person but you. I know the smell of your clothes and the rustle of them. Also your exact light footstep in the gravel. You came. Did you want to make sure I am still alive? You did not speak. Does this mean there is somebody else out there, somebody I can not hear who watches you?

Can it be that Gabriel thinks he should be the second bridegroom and not me? How long has he been given to press his claim? Why did I not make some record of the days? Have I been here a week? On a sudden I need to know. But this is madness, he has nothing in his head but clouds. Forget my foolish worries.

I heard your clothes brush against the wall. The aching in this body of mine, this stranger, kept me awake. An agony of hardness shivered through me. I trembled so much with unspoken thunder I had to cling to the lamp hook by both hands. To be outspoken, convulsions shook me. The cordial shot right across the room, on and on, so that had I been as calm as now I must have feared some damage to my health. It left me feeble.

Do you wonder if I dare not think about your lips. I am in alarm at the power you have over me. There is so much to learn—and I dare be open with you—such adventure. I shake when I think about that tender hidden passage into the life you are keeping secret for me.

I heard your clothes brush the wall and I cried out to you. Yet I was glad you did not come back. How could I have cleaned myself? When we are lovers we will not be shut away or seek shelter. Let us wander the hills and be free of shame. I plan to take you to a pool where we may bathe together. We shall eat oysters and periwinkles. On our journey inland I can find you parrot eggs.

Let my voice work in your mind. Do you hear it repeat and repeat: I love you? By a mercy there was no time for adding anything. This was all you had of me. Your brain can not repeat it more times than I cry it now in here.

Your ever loving lover.

Dearest of all. I find feverous relief in writing another letter. Here is a tale from a book I read. A young man travelling by foot in ancient times met a ghost woman. Of course she was lovely and she welcomed him. She took him to her house, where the chairs were plated with gold. He was a quiet fellow not given to pursuing his lusts, therefore he had made himself helpless against love. He stayed a day or two, a week or two, and at last he married her. Among the friends at the wedding was one with skill to see her for what she was and to see that her golden chairs were no more solid than reflections in water. When the friend spoke to her of this she ranted and stormed, she commanded him to hold his tongue. But he would not. He spoke out until all her gold, her house and she herself vanished as vapour. Thousands of people were witness to the fact of it.

But the book gave no answer to the question I wanted put: Was the young man cured of love or did this leave him worse afflicted than before?

Such love is more terrible than anything. I look at where I am. I count folded blankets. I toy with knives. I stack my written papers ready. I can not bear to think of all the truth I have put in them, or of you opening me as a book. Even the midday light is too dim today and my eyes too full and sore to read.

Where is the justice? You despise me without knowing

me, without hearing what I have to say. As dogged as justice, as prejudiced as the law, you cast me in exile here. So long I have been waiting in this coop, patient because I know you are out there. Am I wrong to have taken your watching for interest? Are you more coward than curious?

Gabriel heard me this morning. He did not run away. He tried to work out the bolt. And at last I lost hope. I told him how to do it. Good soul he did his best. He panted at the task an hour at least before he gave up and prowled around the place. He came back again and again to the puzzle. So someone else locked me in.

I have left myself trapped by my own evil, afire with shame. Does this please your cruelty? Well, let me also confess that even when I am heaping the vilest curses on you my desire is kindled.

The rain begins again. The sea beats up. Think of me and my freedom when you come to look at the splintered roof. This is the best way out, the walls are too thick. I am claiming my freedom and you are to be thanked for it. Whether you wished to tame my spirit or betray me to the courts I do not need to know. The treachery would be the same. You see I have regained the full power of speech.

Your silence itself has become a routine: that is what gives you away.

Suppose I am wrong . . . then you need only set foot

in the wild. The tremendous shock of it will widen like ripples on a pool to be felt for miles around and I shall easy find you. All you must do is hazard starvation or hazard chancing upon some sight not meant for females.

My last folly being sentiment, I still hope.

My dear despair,

Remember this: I am a convicted forger proud of my forgery.

Ought I to sign myself your slave? I would be shortsighted indeed! I begin to suspect you have little sense of humour.

The point is that the forger dedicates his skill to worthless labour. Does this mean that you forgive me because, in the end, my crime was against myself? Meanwhile, I have this to be proud of—that I did not fall into the evil habit of niceness.

To hell with the Psalmist praying: Lord, let me know mine end.

Life will not be trapped in boxes. These letters themselves, after all, my dear, might be forgeries! The end will always come as a surprise.

The rain has stopped. I think of all the clouds swarming into Gabriel's emptiness. What if he sees more beauty in the sky than you do? Unbearable thought.

Mrs Atholl,

I am in terror that you are dead. Gabriel is back. He heard my axe. Read everything. I shall escape as soon as he is out of the way. Read it all.

P.S. My last hope is that you have wished to drive me away to freedom.

To Mrs. Atholl.

Madam,

I have done as instructed. I have read these papers from beginning to end, and a disagreeable task it has been. I shall not set out to enumerate the contents, enough to acknowledge that you were right to suspect this of being a confession. It is indeed. You may recall, Madam, there was a fellow escaped the day we first landed here. At that time your late husband—God rest him—said we were better off to let him go and be rid of a man who would not stop at murder, because anyhow he was sure to die in such wild country. Well, the author of these papers is the self same person but, I fear, still at large. His confession being so perfectly brazen and circumstantial, I believe this whole affair is become a matter for the authorities.

There is, I would suggest, if I may be permitted, little

need for you to bother yourself with the actual papers, all the more so as they are filled with viciousness and indecencies from which I consider it my duty to protect a lady. I must confess that there are also threats made here against your person, which I am convinced you would find distasteful. However, I am firmly of the opinion that the new Governor, Sir George Gipps, must be indebted to you if you was to dispatch the letters direct to him with a request for action. He is doubtless in need of information on the behaviour of such villains, the more so if there be any truth in the rumours I heard in Sydney that he is determined upon being soft with the convicts; also for the assurance that he will find courageous settlers like yourself in the colony whom he may consult and upon whom he can rely as the backbone of society.

Accordingly, Mrs. Atholl, I have packed all the papers and sealed them with wax ready to be sent to Sydney. For the rest, Madam, I venture to suggest that an accompanying letter from yourself ought to secure the matter; in this case I do not doubt that you shall see redcoats arrive here to make an arrest as soon as they can be sent. Indeed, why should His Excellency not consider establishing a small garrison in the district for the protection of British rights, exactly as I have heard you say you wish to see it?

Your obedient and obliged servant,

Wm. Earnshaw

From Mrs. Edwin Atholl,
"Yandilli",
New South Wales.

March 12, 1838.

Your Excellency,

I take the liberty of sending you the inclosed papers to confirm the report sent by my late husband in July of the year before last, concerning the escape of a convict assigned our service. I write also to intreat you to occasion a patrol being despatched down this way to effect the capture of this criminal, who remains still at large, beyond doubt being succoured by savages.

Should you consent to deal summarily with them, which is the savages, I doubt not but they'ld yield him up. Thereby your action would serve the double purposes of bringing a miscreant to justice and punishing his protecters for murdering my husband (also eleven of our assigned workingmen, two pigs, half a dozen sheep, a heffer and an *excellent* bloodhorse), also the distruction of our fences and our farmhouse, also the kitchen and outbuildings which were burnt in the fire—not to mention the spearing of a paid servant and the unknown fate of two others.

I dare persist that I still hope to see the object of my desires fullfilled as my farm flourishes, to produce grain and timber for the betterment of our colony. To this end, I beg you, make haste with re-inforcements for the assigned workmen who are due to arrive here shortly. The truth is that I mistrust the suitability of convicts to be given arms, in consideration of their past crimes. I await your speedy decision.

Meanwhile, kindly permit me to explain about these accompanying papers and how I came by them.

To go back to our catastrophy—well after the fire the quartermaster and our few remaining men sailed our brig, the "Fraternity", to report the tradgedy and the savage character of the blacks in this district. Then he was to fetch help and a fresh assignment of labour to replace those killed.

When the "Fraternity" sailed I watched her out of sight. I shall not attempt to speak of the fears in my breast, nor the *resolution*. I could not face the journey, as I suffer "mal de mer" to an appalling degree. Three servants remained with me, also a harmless creature, Gabriel Dean, a convict who is maimed and has lost his wits, but fond of me and *devoted* to my service. We five were to make a start on the task of rescuing what could be rescued and setting in order those articles left to me—which by great good fortune encluded our store room filled with provisions and tools. However, the very next evening when the poor half-witted creature went missing, two of the servants set out to look for him. They did not return. I went out myself, armed with my husband's best piece. When I returned, with my skirt covered in burrs and my face scratched, I found the third servant dead of a wound to the neck.

To be brief, day after day I called to the missing souls. I risked lighting a fire in the hope that my smoke might guide them back to me; but naturally this put me in fear for my life on the mischance of the blacks being far more likelier to see it instead. I took to concealing myself in a cave which I knew of, down near the jetty a half mile from the house.

Your Excellency, you may imagine how *flabberghasted* I was when, four days later, on the Tuesday, Gabriel Dean imerged from the woods beyond the sawpit, dragging a naked creature by the arm!

I observed their actions from my hiding place. To be frank, I was in terror of being seen, as you may imagine, yet taking care to check that my powder was dry and my weapons stood ready. I should explain that I have salvaged several guns and a pistol. There was still no sign of the two servants who had been sent in search of him—and indeed they have never been seen since.

The convict dragged his captive along the road towards the farm ruin, a creature fighting and struggling the intire way. So soon as they were lost to view round the bend, I creept down and followed, but only so far as I need go to obtain sight of the place. This fellow, Dean, did not let go until they reached the store room, which as I have said miraculously survived the fire, and there the loyal soul locked him in.

I still could not be sure of Dean's intentions so I thought it prudant to retreat to my hiding place. There began my vigil. My first fear was that the good Dean would turn on me too. In this I did him a grave misjudgement. My next fear was that the creature, having plenty of tomahawks in there, would chop his way out and then come after me. Such is the life of a lady in the colonies! I am blessed, I am happy to say, with a strong constitution—my one weakness being, as I have explained, that I fall seasick the moment I set foot in a boat. Even so, I felt under some considerable threat.

The dilema was that I could see he was a white man! Naturally I debated the justice of keeping him inprisoned, also the legal point, lest he might be merely a survivor from some legitimate enterprize, a wrecked ship maybe, perhaps even being a gentleman driven to wildness.

Strange things have been known in this colony, as you will discover when you have been here longer.

Some days elapsed, I must say, before I decided to take

my life in my hands and go down to question Gabriel Dean as to whether or not the prisoner still lived and where my servants might be. I should point out, Your Excellency, that this Dean neither can speak nor clearly be said to understand. Communication with him is difficult. The fact is, however, that he greeted me with touching pleasure and led me to the store, where he slapped the bolt with his hand (he only has one), giving me to understand that his answer regarding the prisoner was positive.

I returned to the store hut several times during the next week. But I dared not let the prisoner out. I feared him dead almost as much as I feared him alive.

Still no relief had arrived, there was not a sign of any sail, and neither of my helpers returned. I began to grow desparate with the worry and responsibility, at a time when I already felt that, in justice, my burden was heavy enough and the task confronting me arduous almost beyond hope of success.

Once when I listened at the wall of the store a voice within uttered an awful cry. It was the roar of a wild beast shouting amorous words which I'ld blush to record.

Who may not imagine the *confusion* of my predicament, the terror, the relief that I did not have the fellow's life on my conscience—or the outrage and the *nausea* at his sentiment? One issue at least had been answered: this was no gentleman. I decided my most prudant course was to take vittals and water again to my hiding place, keep myself armed against mischance or siege, and wait out the perilous days until the servants returned or the quartermaster brought the "Fraternity" home.

The prudance of this plan being confirmed by an onset of drenching rain, I began the last stage of my vigil.

One farther difficulty which I beg to lay before Your Excellency was the necessity of keeping Gabriel Dean ignorant of where I hid, for evidant reasons of decency. I prayed that he might at least take shelter from the rain, also that he had learned to cup his hands to drink from. Convict though he was, and wretched in the extreme, it *wrung my heart* to watch him down there wandering back and forth, desparate for some person to have the charity to take care of his simple needs. My worst fear was that he would find the means to open the bolt in order to have the naked fellow for company.

Strange as it may seem—and perhaps unaccountable viewed from the comfort of a Sydney parlour—when the ship returned I *missed seeing it*, so sunken was I in misery. The pinnace had already put out and nearly reached the jetty before I heard voices hailing me across the water.

I gave thanks to GOD ALMIGHTY for my delivrance.

Now, if I may be permitted the liberty, Sir George, I ought to warn you against a *perilous* tendancy in our colony to indulge the convicts. My late husband, I regret to admit, was guilty of this, although a good man in other respects. You are new to New South Wales and I am convinced you will not take amiss the concern of your conscientious free settlers that you should be made aware of the true issues.

I resolved to establish a new order of strictness now that the task of working the property had fallen to me. In this I am given *great* strength by precious memories of meeting Mrs. John Macarthur, whose fame will doubtless be known to you, as it is in *Westminster*. Mrs. Macarthur successfully conducted bussiness at Camden during her worthy husband's several *long* absences to further their case in the old country, and I trust she is still hale and healthy.

It affords me satisfaction to be able to report that, carrying a musket, I found strength to go down to meet the pinnace and insist upon the quartermaster's arresting the next man to show any such *disorderliness* as to feel free to shout for me! I felt it only fair to be clear that they were under a new regimen. Also I took the precaution of giving orders that the newly assigned convicts were to remain in chains for the time being, until duties could be allotted them, also that the lash should be employed against the least disobedience. This done, we went very quietly in company to inspect the condition of my prisoner—I having apprized the quarter-master (William Earnshaw, by name) of the crisis.

To put it shortly, Your Excellency, it is my duty to report that we came upon the convict Dean laid out dead among his blankets. We could find no sign of struggle. It appears that he crawled on to his rude bedding, which he had piled in one corner of a half-demolished shed, being apparently in some extremity, and died there.

As for the prisoner in the store, the long and the short

of it is that he was gone without trace. He is still at large.

You will be wanting to hear about our stores, which we had been so grateful to find saved from the fire. I confess to having been somewhat amazed when we looked into the hut. We found no damage, apart from a panel of the roof partly smashed, a barrel of biscuits broken open, and a hogshead of grog with the spicket knocked out. The several blankets evidantly removed for use were folded neatly enough and returned where they belonged. The place stank of the fellow's bodily neccessities, yet he had done what he could to conceal this inconvenience. A suit of brown holland clothing, soiled, was placed on a stool beside the table, while upon the table itself we found a sheaf of papers.

I could not bring myself to *touch* anything so insanitary. The place reaked like a sewer. At the thought of his labouring over these papers and fingering them . . . not to put it too indelicately . . . I declined to have the least truck with such filthy stuff. However, I did glance at the top sheet, enough to be surprized by the fair hand it was writ in. For the rest I desired Mr. Earnshaw to look them through.

Having apprized himself of what they contained, he reports that they ammount to a full confession by the escaped convict, who did indeed survive among the savages and by their help. As it seems, on Mr. Earnshaw's insistence, to be a matter of some consequence to your administration during these troubled times, I venture to pass this packet on for your perusal.

My one hope is that such vicious confessions might stir the spirits of those among your staff reputedly under suspicion of showing indulgance towards proven offenders.

Lastly, Sir, to do justice to my own danger, I should point out that the savages in these parts must already be armed with modern weapons. Allthough my late husband was speared three times during the attack, spear wounds did not account for his death. He died of a bullet in the head. I saw the injury for myself. I was not able to write officially of this before dispatching our ship for re-inforcements, owing to the emergency and the *extremity* of my need, not to mention how beside myself I was with *grief*. But I confirmed this highly disturbing development when, with the servants, I buried him.

May I, in closing, Sir George, reassure you that I give no weight whatsoever to rumours that you yourself incline to softness, either towards the savages or the convicts, nor that you would be party to the iniquitous suggestion of imposing land taxes on the very pioneers who are risking their lives to open the country to a great future.

I should like to extend you my warmest congratulations upon your appointment as Governor of New South Wales and trust that you will take *expeditious* action in the matter of establishing the Rule of Law to prevent and discourage mutiny in new districts such as ours.

Ever very truly yours,

Mrs. Edwin Atholl

P.S. A firm stand in the matter of keeping felons in control becomes especially urgent here, as I hear that a convicted person, having a ticket-of-leave, has arrived to take up the neighbouring property, an Irishman with the confidance to call his selection "Paradise", if you please!